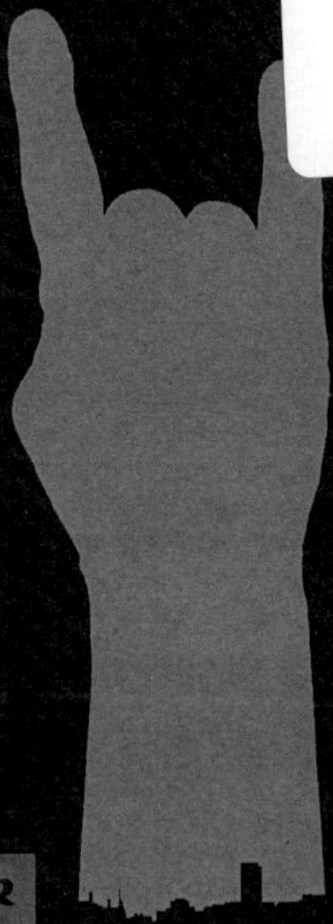

wapentake bar

REBELS

SIGNING ON FOR THE DEVIL

THE RISE OF STEEL CITY ROCK

NEIL ANDERSON

STARRING:

DEF LEPPARD
SAXON
BAILEY BROTHERS
BRUCE DICKINSON
PANZA DIVISION
GEDDES AXE

10TH ANNIVERSARY SPECIAL EDITION

ISBN: 978-1-908431-72-1

Every effort has been made to trace the
copyright holders of photographers in this book
but one or two were unreachable.
We would be grateful if the photographers
concerned would contact us.

Published by ACM Retro 2020.

A catalogue record for this book is available
from the British Library.

www.dirtystopouts.com

Inside Rebels Nightclub.

Pic by Bill Stephenson

Inside Rebels. Pics by Bill Stephenson

STEEL CITY ROCKERS. ALL PICTURES KINDLY SUPPLIED BY SHIRLEY FREEMAN.
VENUES INCLUDE THE PENTHOUSE, STARS, WAPENTAKE AND REBELS

ROKKA

PUSH BAR TO OPEN
STATUS Quo

Hollywood

Contents

Introduction P7

Chapter 1 — Olga Marshall, Trust House Forte and a pact with the Devil P11

Chapter 2 — Wapentake Bar rises from the ashes of a shipwrecked Buccaneer

Chapter 3 — Glitter, Saxon and a future NWOBHM drumming powerhouse

Chapter 4 — We fought the States and we won - Def Leppard P45

Chapter 5 — From mining to MTV mega-stars – The Bailey Brothers P59

Chapter 6 — A Virgin on The Moor – Iron Maiden finds a true number for its beast

Chapter 7 — Rebellion finds a home on Dixon Lane P79

Chapter 8 — All glammed up and somewhere to go – Barry Noble's own altar of metal

Chapter 9 — Seminal gigs and metal marauders from around the region P113

Chapter 10 — Other rock hits, misses and metal notables P123

Chapter 11 — Ten years later – gone but not forgotten P144

Pete Gill (second from left) back stage at Port Vale's Heavy Metal Holocaust with Lemmy (left) and then 'Fast' Eddie Clarke (fourth from right), Ozzy Osbourne, Tommy Aldridge and Phil 'Philthy Animal' Taylor.

Rocking from the edge of the grunge abyss – two of the more colourful regulars at Sheffield City Hall's Drop night in the 1990s

Intro

Rock music was having a pretty tortuous existence in the latter half of the 1970s.

It was all sweetness and light in the early part of the decade with the likes of Led Zeppelin, Deep Purple and Black Sabbath rising to prominence.

But by 1976 a decidedly unwelcome guest had gate-crashed the party in the shape of punk rock.

Heavy metal had no choice but to go underground and it was down to a close-knit group to fight for its place in the upper echelons of Sheffield nightlife.

The battle was led by one Shirley Freeman whose tenacity you've got to more than admire. She was chairperson of the Penthouse Action Committee (PAC) that fought tooth and nail for the scene they so loved.

She also went armed with something nearly as valuable as tenacity in the mid-1970s – a camera.

Castle Market's Penthouse was one of the first nightclubs in the city to start playing rock music.

It started to get a foothold in the years following the departure of Peter and Geoff Stringfellow – the brothers that originally opened the venue in 1969.

But when soul music started to encroach on nights normally given over to rock music the group of regulars decided – in true 1970s style – to make a stand.

PAC lobbied the management and were so successful they soon got their rock nights re-instated.

They went on to campaign for an improved sound system and staged early gigs by the likes of Def Leppard and Rokka.

PAC – consisting of Shirley Freeman, Mick Cassidy, Jenny Jones, Della Freeston, Jackie Ball, Larry Massey and DJ Bob Maltby – also went on to stage

ALL GLAMMED UP AND READY TO ROCK – LEADING LIGHTS FROM SHEFFIELD'S FEMALE ROCK FRATERNITY

regular rock nights at Stars on Queens Road after the Penthouse changed direction and turned into Dollars speakeasy.

Maybe it was the region's inability to produce any first rate punk bands that opened the doors to the likes of Def Leppard.

Whatever the reason, the city's sonic twist on the then floundering rock movement helped produce some of its key exponents of the early 1980s.

Sheffield's early adoption of a new, and far more exciting manifestation of the rock scene was that significant it even attracted The Guardian to do a massive feature on heavy metal life at Wapentake Bar - one of the city's main rock haunts - as far back as 1980.

They reported: "Heavy metal has been, and probably always will be, strongest in bleak industrial towns. Sheffield is one of those places where it never really went away: the Wapentake has been playing the same music since 1973. Now Sheffield has its local heavy metal heroes. A group of teenagers formed a

"Heavy metal has been, and probably always will be, strongest in bleak industrial towns. Sheffield is one of those places where it never really went away: the Wapentake has been playing the same music since 1973. Now Sheffield has its local heavy metal heroes. A group of teenagers formed a group called Def Leppard there two years ago and ended up in the charts."
The Guardian, 1980.

DEF LEPPARD

group called Def Leppard there two years ago and they ended up in the charts."

The band became key exponents of the New Wave Of British Heavy Metal movement alongside stablemates Saxon from nearby Barnsley (with Sheffield's own Pete Gill behind the drums) together with a rejuvenated Iron Maiden, led by Bruce Dickinson who was born in Worksop and schooled in Sheffield.

And despite major twists in the rock genre throughout the following decade, including the rise of glam and thrash, Sheffield held its own – in fact it's fair to say Def Leppard

REBELS' DJS (LEFT TO RIGHT) KEN HALL, BOB MALTBY AND LEZ WRIGHT

SEX PISTOLS AT RADIO HALLAM IN 1976 – THE BAND THAT KILLED PROG ROCK

had more than a little influence in the rise of softer rock that led to new audiences being attracted to the scene for the first time.

But it wasn't just the music that was influenced by Sheffield.

The Steel City changed the face of heavy metal dance floors the world over when The Bailey Brothers, two ex-miners from Sheffield, inadvertently invented the air guitar and wowed crowds right across the UK and Europe with a outlandish mix of cutting edge metal, cardboard guitars and pyrotechnics.

Their massive influence helped break major US rock acts in the UK – they were the first DJs to play the likes of Bon Jovi and scores of others and even boasted their own chart in weekly music bible, Sounds.

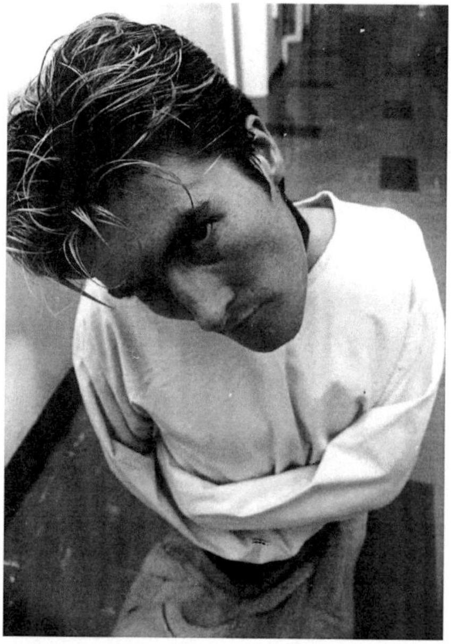

JOHNNY LOCO FITTED OUT IN FETCHING STRAITJACKET FRESH FROM HIS SHEFFIELD CITY HALL BAN FOR HIS BAND ETIQUETTE

THE HIGH PRIESTESS OF HEAVY METAL – OLGA MARSHALL IN RESIDENCE AT WAPENTAKE BAR

Saxon went on to be one of the key inspirations for spoof rockumentary 'This Is Spinal Tap' before Pete Gill disappeared to inject Sheffield metal into Lemmy's Motörhead and take over drumming duties.

Back in Sheffield, hundreds were packing out rock clubs like Rebels on Dixon Lane and making Sheffield City Hall a true Northern stronghold for touring big metal bands.

Rock matriarch, the legendary Olga Marshall, kept the metal-heads happy in her renowned Wapentake Bar whilst Barry Noble's Roxy glammed it up like never before at their regular Monday night bash that attracted punters from all over Northern England and further afield. Sheffield – we salute you!

Chapter 1

Olga Marshall, Trust House Forte and a pact with the Devil

Olga Marshall

Though it's arguable that Sheffield's rock scene was never at its true height until the mid 1980s, its roots can be traced back at least two decades as far as one of the main flagbearers was concerned.

Olga Marshall became a legend as the formidable face of the sprawling cellar bar that became a byword for the city's metal scene, Wapentake Bar.

It's fair to say that the future fairy godmother of the Sheffield rock scene, or Wapentake Bar itself for that matter, couldn't have been more unlikely candidates for either of their future roles.

The venue itself was owned by prim and proper hotel chain Trust House Forte – hardly a company with a world beating record in the rock bar department.

Olga herself was a virtual teetotal mother of four and would have probably looked more at home running an upmarket guesthouse than a downtown den of rock'n'roll iniquity.

But ran it she did and her no nonsense approach was even heeded by the local Hells Angels chapters who became model citizens under her watch.

Olga Marshall's dominance on the city's after dark scene actually started as far back as 1964 when even future rock music trailblazers like Led Zeppelin, Black Sabbath and Deep Purple were still years from forming.

She landed a job as a barmaid at the Buccaneer – a set of themed bars sited under the Grand Hotel which used to sit on Sheffield's Leopold Street.

It's fair to say the owners – Trust House Forte once again – had never figured on their nautical-themed venue being turned into a bastion of alternative rock sounds.

But they didn't figure on the headstrong world of Olga Marshall whose influence was felt from day one.

The venue's music policy was one of the first things she wanted changing to help draw in more punters.

Olga Marshall said: "We'd only got a jukebox so I spoke to the management company about getting a DJ in. They brought in a company called DRM who came along with flashing lights and the full set-up but they just weren't what we wanted at all.

"I asked if I could sort something out myself and I found George Webster, who was playing at Cannon Hall social club at Page Hall [Sheffield] at the time, and he started playing the kind of music that my customers liked."

Her success that night sealed her fate and started a metallic ball rolling that was to last over three decades...

"We took more on our first night with George than the Buccaneer took on its average weekend", she proudly said.

The Buccaneer became one of the city's busiest venues with Olga at the helm. The venue was a massive concern with around 60 staff. The Buccaneer was also ideally placed to serve the punters on the way to the nearby Sheffield City Hall – a venue that was already securing landmark gigs by the bands that were shaping the fast developing rock movement.

The concert venue's ticket outlet, Wilson Peck Ltd, was also sited next door to the Buccaneer.

Fans were quite happy to queue all night to ensure they landed tickets for Led Zeppelin in one of their early gigs in Sheffield.

Buccaneer in action

Buccaneer assistant manager Norman Coldwell (left) and DJs George Webster (centre) and Ian Roberts

Olga Marshall soon became a regular fixture in the local press and her venue became the stuff of legend.

Buccaneer Bar regular Peter Eales said: "The Buccaneer had a true aura of rebellion. There was nowhere else playing music like it in Sheffield.

"You went to the Buccaneer if you wanted to hear stuff that was different, that wasn't mainstream. There were lots of different rooms but it was that dark you could never tell where you were anyway."

Unfortunately the nautical rock'n'roll action wasn't to last.

Trust House Forte sold the site for redevelopment and, despite outlasting the Grand Hotel upstairs which was bulldozed and replaced by an office block a few weeks earlier, The Buccaneer shut its doors for the last time in 1973 after 1,979 days of custom. The clientele were absolutely distraught.

Aware of the widespread dismay at the thought of closure among the hardcore following, the management made the decision to close the bars without warning in a bid to stop souvenir hunters.They failed.

The Sheffield Star reported the police were looking for four missing tables soon after it shut.

We can solve the mystery of one – it still sits proudly in Olga Marshall's garage alongside the pub sign.

Olga has no idea where the other three ended up...

Buccaneer in action

CRAZY DAIZY PAVES THE WAY FOR WAPENTAKE BAR

The Sheffield rock scene was virtually stopped in its tracks with the shock closure of the Buccaneer. Many of the punters decamped to the Crazy Daizy venue on High Street but its Roxy Music nights and early adoption of punk rock never really did it for the rockers.

The venue ended up achieving legendary status as the club in which Human League front man Phil Oakey first clapped eyes on Joanne Catherall and Susan Sulley, who went on to complete his new-look band and go on to global domination.

Dixon Lane's Penthouse venue, which later became rock venue Rebels and was originally opened by Peter Stringfellow in 1969, became a popular rock haunt by the mid-1970s but by the time the Buccaneer Bar shut it was still developing and wasn't an automatic alternative.

The saviour for the rockers, bizarrely, came along in the shape of Trust House Forte once agan

The saviour for the rockers, bizarrely, came along in the shape of Trust House Forte once again with more than a little help by a slightly older and wiser Olga Marshall.

She'd been summoned to the company's Wapentake Bar, a venue sited underneath their Charter Square Grosvenor House Hotel, which was, at the time, underperforming in a similar way to the Buccaneer in its days before Olga Marshall.

The venue was a definite Jekyll and Hyde character in the early days of Olga.

It was renowned as a lunch haven for shop and office workers and only developed, a few months into Olga's watch, as a rock venue by night.

After a few weeks of browbeating by Olga, Trust House Forte management allowed George "Buccaneer" Webster – as he was billed at the time - and his rock music to become the new weapon of choice for the Wapentake Bar after dark residents.

Management at the Grosvenor House Hotel were actually eager to do their bit to help welcome their new rock crowd in the early days.

"The hotel manager, Mr Tallis, suggested we ought to have a party for the rockers and he offered to lay on some jelly," said Olga.

"I told him not to be so stupid. He did take his suit off one night, came down in a T-shirt and told me: 'Your crowd are actually alright to talk to.' I'm not quite sure what he expected!"

As with the Buccaneer Bar, as the takings increased, interference from the hotel upstairs decreased.

The Wapentake Bar, without a shadow of a doubt, went on to become one of the most legendary metal destinations on the UK music map.

Chapter 2

Wapentake Bar rises from the ashes of a shipwrecked Buccaneer

Wapentake DJ and future Limit DJ Paul Unwin

Few people ever associated the then swish Grosvenor House Hotel (the place still survives today but is ear-marked for demolition to make way for a heavily delayed shopping precinct) on Charter Square roundabout in Sheffield city centre as the owners of the Wapentake Bar.

It probably worked better that way: only the management and a few others knew the two were inherently linked, it would have done little for the street cred of either operation had the situation been widely publicised.

The Wapentake Bar had its own entrance well out of view of the hotel and you had to descend a flight of stairs before you got so much as a sniff of the action.

Décor was – at best – basic; it had a very low ceiling and the place was sweaty and dark.

The punters couldn't have been happier and the place was soon running six nights a week and was also promoting regular gigs - Def Leppard played one of their first ever outings down there.

There was rarely trouble, despite the venue's appeal to biker gangs who the

WAPENTAKE REGULARS

DJ Ken Hall, Olga Marshall and John Alflat

firm hand of Olga Marshall always managed to control.

It was always renowned for its almost 'family atmosphere'.

But the Wapentake Bar was always firmly rock and, though they used to frequent the place, it never had the same resonance for the punks and new wave fraternity which started appearing from 1976.

Paul Unwin, the Wapentake Bar DJ who went on to make his name as resident DJ at legendary West Street venue The Limit, said: "In the mid seventies we did begin to move away from rock with the advent of punk. I can remember the landlady Olga Marshall taking exception to the fact that people were turning up dressed in bin bags with little bum flaps."

"I can remember the landlady Olga Marshall taking exception to the fact that people were turning up dressed in bin bags with little bum flaps."

DJ Paul Unwin

Paul argues, like many, that the music scene needed freshening up.

He said: "For me it was the way forward. I was only 21 but the music scene was really beginning to excite me again. It had been in a bit of a trough after 1972 because it went into the glam stages of Bolan and Sweet while hard rock acts like Deep Purple and Led Zeppelin played music of the same quality as they'd done previously."

Nobody could fail to miss the amount of money the Wapentake Bar was turning over – it was, like the Buccaneer – a formidable operation on the Sheffield bar scene.

OLGA'S OFFER TO JUMP SHIP

Things could have been different for the city's rock scene in 1977 with the punk scene going begging.

The Wapentake resident DJ George Webster, alongside punter and former policeman Kevan Johnson, decided there was more of a future in punk and secured the West Street premises that became The Limit.

They asked Olga Marshall if she fancied jumping ship and running the new operation being planned.

She said: "I didn't know anything about it until George Webster asked to see me one night and asked if I wanted to come and work for him," said Olga.

"I said no – the hours were too late. I liked pub hours rather than the 2am of nightclubs and said I wanted to stay at the Wapentake Bar."

There was little to rival its size and reputation in terms of rock bars in the country

Thousands upon thousands of rockers over the next two decades were thankful she stayed.

Regular Ian Cheetham said: "The Wapentake Bar became an absolute magnet for rockers – if you were in Sheffield you had to go to The Wap. I was a punter there for nearly two decades and nobody could believe it was run by this smartly dressed mother of four who took no nonsense from anyone – Hells Angels or anyone."

Olga Marshall's proudest moment was probably a return visit by Def Leppard, who performed for her one more time at the Wapentake Bar on October 5, 1995, in front of most of the world's music press (one unfortunate member of staff felt the wrath of Olga for refusing to book the band second time around claiming 'we don't put live music on anymore' – the mistake was quickly rectified).

There was little to rival its size and reputation in terms of rock bars in the country.

And definitely little to rival the women at its helm, Olga Marshall.

It was a formidable force and became the mainstay of the rockers' Sheffield pub circuit that would also include the likes of The Yorkshireman, The Nelson, The Sportsman and other venues over the years.

It was also a landing pad for rockers from nearby towns like Chesterfield, Rotherham, Barnsley and Doncaster and further afield who would meet there before heading down to Rebels rock club on Dixon Lane.

Newcastle Brown was consumed by the lorry load, the music was of a volume to shake the building's very foundations but, despite its hard exterior, it had a largely trouble-free existence.

DJ LEZ WRIGHT

The venue was definitely the backbone of the whole scene.

Its reputation, and that of the burgeoning Sheffield rock scene as a whole, even came to the attention of The Guardian as far back as 1980.

They did a massive spread on the place and even sent photo legend Denis Thorpe to capture proceedings in long-haired, denim and leather-wearing, subterranean Sheffield.

Reporter Mary Harron said: "The Wapentake is a modern pub in the centre of Sheffield, as anonymous as any other, but in the evenings it is like a secret clubhouse. The regulars are nearly all in their late teens or early twenties, and they come for one reason: to hear the heavy metal records that the resident DJ plays all night at ear-shattering volume.

"Subtlety has no place in heavy metal. Critics have called it the worst form of rock music ever invented, but no form of rock music ever invented inspires such passionately devoted fans; the success of heavy metal is the phenomenon of the year in British rock."

The reporter was more than a little stunned at events kicking off on the dance floor.

"The DJ announced a single by Iron Maiden and, as the music pounded, three teenage boys entered what looked like a slow-motion epileptic fit. Eyes closed in ecstasy, they jerked their heads back and forth in time, fingers strumming imaginary electric guitars. No one in the room batted an eye-lid."

She also tries to explain its strong bond with Sheffield when she said: "Heavy metal has been, and probably always will be, strongest in bleak industrial towns. Sheffield is one of those places where it never really went away: the Wapentake has been playing the same music since 1973. Now Sheffield has its local heavy metal heroes. A group of teenagers formed a group called Def Leppard there two years ago and ended up in the charts."

The Wapentake regular quoted in the piece said the band had already fallen into disfavour.

He said: "They're a Sheffield band but they've just grown too big. They've sold out. Well they've gone to America, haven't they?"

He signs off by saying the band would never be playing the Wapentake again. He was wrong. They returned to their old stomping ground in 1995.

Def Leppard, it has to be said, did inadvertently manage to develop a love/hate relationship with rockers in the UK in their early years – things are rather more chilled out these days.

An infamous appearance at Reading Festival in 1980 saw the band greeted with a hail of cans and bottles after the crowd were convinced the band had turned their back on them in favour of the States.

That, by all accounts, was pretty chilled out compared to events backstage.

Chris Twiby said: "On the Reading campsite, what started out as a joke got a bit out of hand. This involved my uncle and 4/5 mates (who hated Leppard) who went round asking who liked the band. Anybody who said yes got dragged out of their tent and thrown into the river. What started off as a Pythonesque laugh soon escalated, the mob got bigger and a bit out of hand, a few bikers got involved and it ended up where any Leppard lover was dragged through the mud, roughed up and thrown in the water. Some young couple (naked) were in the middle of 'something' and he was dragged off, still naked, and held under the water until he said Def Leppard were shit. Even a bloke on crutches with a pot on his leg was not spared. They ended up tipping cars over and trying to roll them into the river...the police put a stop to it all eventually. All that for selling out to America..."

Def Leppard were also flanked by bands that were very much in favour that year

Def Leppard were also flanked by bands that were very much in favour that year.

Chris Twiby said: "The situation was not helped by following a resurgent Slade who went down a storm and having festival favourites Whitesnake in their Brit Blues Pomp headlining (ironically they sold out themselves to the USA years later)."

All has been forgiven 30 years on.

A PLACE FOR PENSIONERS

OLGA MARSHALL (LEFT) DJ GEORGE WEBSTER (FAR RIGHT) AND STAFF COLLECT FOR SHEFFIELD'S OAPS

The Wapentake Bar definitely started life with clientele rather different than the one it ended up with.

Despite turning around the fortunes at the nearby Buccaneer Bar, Olga Marshall was told she had to toe the company line and forget the rockers when she first started in her new venue.

Olga Marshall said of the early days: "We were renowned for serving up homely food – we were very popular with pensioners and shop and office workers. Meat and potato pie was one of our best sellers together with long sausages in breadsticks. We also did cottage pie and salad.

"We became a meeting place for pensioners and served cheap meals. We also became a popular destination for the Telegraph's 'women's circle' for two or three years.

"I teamed up with the Cineplex and, for 99p each, the ladies would get lunch at the Wapentake Bar, a tour of the hotel upstairs and then get to see a film. I'd also sometimes give them sherry from the hotel's cocktail bar."

But the venue was soon taking on bizarre Jekyll and Hyde characteristics as rock started to get a stranglehold in the evenings – a situation only encouraged by Olga Marshall.

JOHN ALFLAT SAID:
"Olga moved to run the Wapentake Bar and after something like a year she brought back a DJ and quickly established it as the place to be if you like heavier type music.
"In those days you had to queue to get in every night apart from Monday or Wednesday.
"I started going down the Wapentake in 1974/1975 and used to go down virtually every night. At the time of Leppard's first gigs I actually worked down there as a glass washer to supplement my day job."

IAN CHEETHAM SAID:
"The Wapentake Bar became an absolute magnet for rockers – if you were in Sheffield you had to go to The Wap. I was a punter there for nearly two decades and nobody could believe it was run by a smartly dressed mother of four who took no nonsense from anyone – Hells Angels or anyone."

DJ LEZ WRIGHT SAID:
"Olga Marshall, the only woman in the world that could hold back an army of Hell's Angels."

DJ LEZ WRIGHT

ALAN HARGREAVES SAID:
"The Wapentake became a melting pot for misfits that couldn't get in anywhere else. Rockers, punks, Hells Angels, Goths, hippies... you name and they were in there."

JACKIE CAPPER SAID:
Jackie Capper said: "I first went into the Wapentake when I was 14. I told my mum I was going to see Queen at the City Hall."

PHIL STANILAND SAID:
"It seemed that if rock music was your calling circa 1978 everything revolved around the Wapentake Bar or 'Wap' (pronounced 'Wop') as it was often referred to. "When you were fresh out of school and had just started college because either you couldn't get a job or you just didn't know what to do it was quite a magical period. This was my position at the time.

"That is why I like The Casbah [the guise of Wapentake Bar today] so much because it reminds me of those halcyon days and because the venue has hardly changed in its appearance I become lost in those memories as soon as I enter. Despite the grim situation as regards one's future outlook back then there seemed to be so much optimism once you had become immersed within this in some ways 'insular' world.

"The records that seem synonymous with this Wapentake period that immediately spring to mind are 'Like a Hurricane' by Neil Young, 'Take Me to the River' by the Talking Heads, several songs from the 'Bat Out of Hell' album by Meatloaf, 'Hit me With Your Rhythm Stick' and 'Sweet Gene Vincent' by Ian Dury, 'Sabbath Bloody Sabbath' by Black Sabbath, 'I Can't Get Enough of Your Love' by Bad Company, and 'Black Night' by Deep Purple. Plus many many more of course but these are the ones that remain stored in my memory banks.

"Despite the grim situation as regards one's future back then there seemed to be so much optimism."

"At the same time the Nelson Pub across from what used to be Redgates toy shop in the '70s was the sister rock venue. The downstairs part was an almost bare and very basic room with huge garish paintings on the wall of David Bowie, Alice Cooper and, I seem to remember, maybe one of Jeff Beck or Rod Stewart. There were a few basic chairs and tables and in a way it resembled a simpler version of the Korova Milk Bar in Stanley Kubrick's classic film 'A Clockwork Orange'. Minus of course the 'female figure' design furniture. The only sound system was a juke box which occupied a space against the wall to the right of the small bar, and which always seemed to be playing constantly.

"Classic rock tracks seemed to be on a permanent loop such as 'All Along the Watchtower' by Hendrix, '21st Century Schizoid Man' by King Crimson, 'The Crystal Ship' and 'Light My Fire' by The Doors, 'Frankenstein' by the Edgar Winter Group, 'I Know What I Like' by Genesis, and 'Rock And Roll' by Led Zeppelin. This is just to mention only a few but these are the ones that instantly spring to mind in hindsight. I spent some good drunken weekends and Christmas's here in the late '70's. These definitely were my 'paralytic' years!!

WAPENTAKE REGULARS

"Every Thursday night when we were out straight from college for a drunken night out it became apparent that the fountain at the top of Fargate (as was) became a hinterland for drunken rockers who seemed to end their evening by doing the backstroke in it while usually wearing an Afghan coat which weren't the lightest of coats. Even Houdini would have struggled trying to emerge from a watery challenge while wearing one of them. I know we always seemed to end up in the fountain and it became commonplace for the police to be fishing rockers out of the fountain after last orders. Anyway those Afghan coats reeked to high heaven even before they had been in the fountain. After being in the fountain a few times they were even worse. I can't even imagine what it must have been like now when I think of a packed Wapentake made up of all those rockers wearing an Afghan that had been in the fountain a few times. The Wapentake was hot inside to start with and those coats must have been designed to combat the conditions of the Antarctic, they made you sweat and were very itchy. The combination of sweat, smell, heat and discomfort must have created a real 'Total Environment Syndrome' to use Warholian terminology. The shop that used to sell them was Pippy's which was on Cambridge Street and just around the corner from the Wapentake.

"Pippy's also supplied 'lived in' second hand biker jackets which is ideally how you wanted them."

"I remember seeing them all hung up outside like dead animals which is what they were I suppose really!! Pippy's also supplied 'lived in' second hand biker jackets which is ideally how you wanted them. They didn't have the same presence when they were new and just looked like they had come out of a mail order catalogue. Ideally you wanted a battered verion that looked like it had been worn in by the likes of Johnny Thunders or Iggy Pop – Pippy's had these in great supply I seem to remember.

"Failing that you had to wear them for years before they got to the aforementioned 'mature' status. What was also good about these jackets is that the inside pockets always used to break and when that happened you could fit anything in them as the pocket space increased. It was like having a built in travel bag. What you could fit in was nobody's business – an umbrella in the event of rain, even an unfinished pint pot or bottles you may have had to smuggle out of the previous pub to take with you to the next place.

"I was once barred from the Wapentake due to a 'seat slashing ' incident which was nothing to do with me and I know that any of the 'accused' who may be reading this will remember it. My college friend Gary Mackender springs to mind as he was one of those that was set up. Basically one Thursday night some of the seats in the alcoves that used to be there then were slashed and the bouncers decided to take matters into their own hands. I'm not sure Olga Marshall would have known about this. I remember one of the bouncers 'Paul' being the ringleader of the 'lynchin' party' as it was. He always reminded me of Steve Jones from the Pistols in his appearance except he had mousy blond hair. Anyway on the following Friday night the bouncers decided to pick at random a few 'easy targets' of which I was one. They took us into the doorway near the toilets and told us we were barred unless we could get the real guilty party to come forward and own up to it. Everyone knew who it was of course and I don't suppose now it would do any harm to name them 30 odd years later - but I won't. Of course we were all mortified as this venue was our lives. Where else would we go to? Anyway everyone of the 'framed' bunch stayed away - but I kept going in. I got lucky on the nights I took the risk as it probably always fell on Paul's night off. However one Thursday night I sneaked in while he was preoccupied with some people in the doorway and proceeded to go and get a round from the bar. As I came back with the round of drinks he spotted me and dragged me out into the doorway and all the beer glasses went into the air. He gave me a bit of a 'leatherin' which I remember being a bit ineffective against the cushioned sedation of the night's cocktail of beer,

DJ KEN HALL

Ken Hall started providing the sounds at Wapentake Bar in 1978.

He said: "George Webster left and went to the Limit but he was still putting DJs on down at the Wapentake. He said he wanted some more DJs so I says 'alright how about me?' 'Well come up to The Limit and audition for me, and I'll see' he said.

"Then he said 'yes, you can start this weekend'. So I walked in, Olga knew me from the Buccaneer days as a regular.

"On a Saturday night, I used to play 'The bucket of water song' about quarter past ten and everyone used to go berserk because everyone used to see it on ITV's 'Tiswas' on a Saturday morning.

"At one point people went up to the bar ordered six pints of bitter when they knew I was putting it on so they could throw them at people. That used to be a riot that."

Ken Hall

DEZ BAILEY SAID:
"The Wapentake is where we first saw a very young Def Leppard performing UFO and Thin Lizzy covers. The ceiling was way too low to get a good sound but Leppard, even then, had a charm and energy about them. We played with them eventually and were really pleased for them when things finally came together. No band in the world deserves to be successful more than our local heroes, especially after all the stuff they have been through. I can remember the famous football game in the corner which an old friend of ours, Frank Cross, would be on all night. He later went on to have one in his house complete with floodlights and juke box.

"You had to queue right down the road to get in the Wap, sometimes you would leg it to the Nelson hoping the queue would have diminished when you got back. The music was a bit dated but the scene was really cool and friendly. Olga ran a really good business there and should be applauded as the Grosvenor House Hotel owners didn't really want a rock pub but loved the takings."

shorts, and whatever else had been consumed. I was only about 17 at the time and Paul was a very stocky and much taller bloke who must have been in his late 20's or 30's. Anyway he carried me up the Wapentake staircase mainly by my chin as I seem to remember, slammed me up against the top wall, and then opened the door and threw me out. It was like the stereotypical drunk being ejected from the saloon scene in a western movie. I came flying out of the door and I landed in the gutter or road edge directly at the side of a very strung out Warlock type smoking a huge spliff that looked like it needed supporting on a rod rest. Totally undeterred he put the joint in front of me and said "Never mind – have a bang at that number man!!!!"

"When I awoke the next day and saw the cuts and bruises I was a bit shocked. It was said on the night in jest that I was targeted, knocked about, and thrown out before the round of drinks I had been carrying hit the floor!!!! It all ended amicably in the end as some time later the seat slashing incident was resolved and the innocent parties were given their season tickets back and were reinstated.

"I remember Paul being a bit edgy when I started going back in and possibly a little pissed off as Olga had given him strict instructions not to touch me or anyone related to the incident. I wonder what ever happened to him. Maybe he may read this one day."

Phil Staniland said: "The Wapentake was a keen promoter of local talent and I remember seeing quite a few bands midweek during the late '70s. The one's that spring to mind are obviously Def Leppard who I also saw at The Penthouse on at least one occasion. At this time their set comprised of their own material plus a few covers and I remember them doing songs like 'Doctor Doctor' by UFO. Others were Glenn Marples's Rokka who seemed to be playing a lot at that time at various venues particularly The Penthouse. One band I'll always remember were 'Fixer' who had a guitarist who dressed like Groucho Marx and had a cherry red Fender Stratocaster. The drummer also used to sit on an old television set as opposed to a proper drum stool. I'd love to hear what they sounded like now as I can't remember much about their music just the characters in the band. The Groucho guy was quite captivating to me at the time - me being a mere young teenage rock fan who was desperate to be playing in a band myself. I never felt I fully fitted in with the rock fraternity at this time as I was more of a New York Dolls and Stooges fan but I did like a lot of classic rock too. I remember seeing Sheffield band 'I'm So Hollow' one Thursday night in the Wapentake who were clearly miscast for this venue as they were the furthest thing from standard rock you could get. I always like them, still do, and 'Touch' by them is still a classic in my book. They were more experimental and very in vogue for the time and would have been more at home at The Limit which I'm sure they would have played. They came from the darker music regions of 'industrial Sheffield'. Gary Marsden provided real menacing bass lines and they had a female singer I seem to remember who was just called 'Wilson' who wore very pale face make up and played a WASP synthesizer. I'd not seen one of these at the time as they were quite new and wondered what it was. It was a kind of cheap toy synthesizer option if you couldn't afford a Mini Moog I suppose and now would probably fetch silly money as these retro instruments do. I suppose around this time if you were a rocker the main (well probably only) three venues were the Wapentake, The Penthouse and The Nelson.

Wapentake regulars

THE WRATH OF THE YORKSHIREMAN

Phil Staniland said: "Nights in The Yorkshireman were fantastic and viewed as very halcyon days by everyone I know who ever went there. During the late '80s it was a good central meeting point for people going on to the Monday Rock Night at Roxy's or Rebels (which could be any night of the week). It was managed by the extremely bad tempered but lovable Mick the landlord who only appeared to like one person that went in and that was my manager at work (when I worked at Sheffield City Council's Photography Department) Chris Calow. He appeared to hate everyone else that went in the pub. I remember once while he was executing one of his mass pint pulling frenzies some glass shattering and jumping up at me as I was at the front of the beer queue. He said in an out of character but caring manner 'did that hit you then?' To which I replied 'no'. Then after he'd served me he told me the total cost of the drinks to which I replied 'Sorry you will have to speak up Mick I'm a bit mutton jeff'. He did just that and I paid him. He must have detected some slight sarcasm because in a quieter voice he pointed down at the bar and said 'is that your fiver there?'

"'Where' I replied looking for the non existent fiver and totally falling for his ploy. It had been clear to him I could hear him all along. His voice then erupted over the volume of the rock

WAPENTAKE REGULARS

music still being played on the twin decks saying 'AAAAAhhhhhhh but ya fuckin heard that ya bastard!!!!!!!' The customer service charter mark wasn't around in those days. If it had been I'm sure that Mick the landlord would have been sent on a rehabilitation course. I wouldn't have wanted him to change though to be honest.

"Mick eventually moved on to be replaced by the more placid and likeable 'Les the Landlord' and The Yorkshireman still continued to thrive. 'Les's Lock In's' on a Saturday night became legendary. If you were one of the lucky few invited back after last orders you waited for the signal outside. When you went back in Les would kick start the proceedings by producing a small (kiddies) cash tin and the juke box light would come back on. You then enjoyed the bonus of two good nights in one!! No club required!!

"The Yorkshireman had been a great venue for people to meet and in most cases 'stay' as you didn't feel the need to move on anywhere else during standard licensing hours as it was such a good scene. It was always busy at weekends and did fairly ok midweek I seem to remember. The jukebox was consistently good and some nights there would be resident DJs there still spinning vinyl combined with the addition of CDs. I have fond memories of times spent during the summer months in the beer garden (or beer yard to be more correct).

"When the venue started to wane and eventually cease its 'rock operations' it sadly split a lot of people up and the rock scene in Sheffield really lost something crucial I felt. The Yorkshireman was taken over by new tenants during the subsequent years who all gave it a major facelift to deter any stray rockers and attract different 'clientele'. Ironically the venue was never really that successful during this time.

"This highlighted the fact that you should never mess with the Wrath of the Yorkshireman!!! It only ever seemed to work with a 'rock' landlord steering the way.

"I think the Knebworth Festival of 1979 has a memorable association with the Wapentake years of the late '70s. I have a vivid memory of the Wapentake being a kind of meeting point for some groups of festival goers. It certainly was for us. This was the year Led Zeppelin headlined and they decided to do two alternate weekends with an attendance of about 200,000 so I heard. This figure is still debatable however.

"At that time I wasn't a big Zeppelin fan but I was a big Stones fan and wanted to see the New Barbarians which was Ronnie Wood's band featuring Keith Richards. They were playing the second weekend (11th August 1979) but I had seen groups of concert goers gathering the week before in The Wapentake for the first concert. Anyway a few of us met in The Wapentake, had a few drinks, and then made a couple more pick ups on the way. The entourage was myself, 'Kang' (Mark Glover), 'Chic' (Dave Murray), Nig ('the driver' derived from Nigel), and Gary Mackender and his girlfriend Jill. We arrived at Knebworth the night before and I recall being directed to a crowded camping area where thousands had set up camp and it had that real Woodstock vibe to it. I remember there being a strong smell of dope all around and someone had got a radio on at maximum volume near us. A live version of 'My Generation' by The Who was playing and I think it was the version they played on the Smothers Brothers show that appeared on the 'Kids Are Alright' album a few years later.

To an impressionable teenager who felt he had missed the '60s this was like a dream come true to me. The entire festival was really great although I can only remember fragments of the Zeppelin performance mainly due to my ignorance of their songs. It took some years for me to really warm to Zeppelin and now I really like them. The Barbarians lived up to expectations and it was just great being able to see two fifths of the Stones.

They played some of the stuff from the album 'Gimme Some Neck' with some Stones songs chucked in as well.

There was something like an hour or two's delay which they said was down to having to show bassist Phil Chen the songs. Chen had been in Rod Stewart's band and more recently Riders on the Storm (The Doors). To quote Ronnie Wood 'he's a quick learner!!!!!!' A few years ago someone told me the 'real reason' for the delay and that it was because Ronnie and Keith were haggling with Zeppelin's manager Peter Grant for the money upfront. Apparently they refused to play if he didn't pay them in cash and there was some story Grant had to go back and get it from the hotel safe. I don't know if this is true but it certainly makes a good rock 'n' roll story. My lasting memory of this festival was right at the end when the field was almost empty. Somehow some of the trees managed to catch fire. It sent a surreal glow over the debris across the field in front of the stage and I saw of few silhouetted people jumping from the lower branches of the trees. It was a real 'moment of clarity'."

MORE LIKE A SOCIAL CLUB

Iain Barker ended up as head doorman at the Wapentake – many moons after he first started frequenting the place. His future wife Mandi was also a regular. They both have fond memories of the place.

He said: "I started going to the Wapentake aged 14. I'd got really long hair so they couldn't tell how old I was which helped.

"In 1980 I started working on the door at Sheffield City Hall. I remember being backstage chatting to The Scorpions and people like that and when the gig finished it would be back down to the Wap.

"It was more like a social club. There were little groups all round the pub but you always knew somebody in each group. The mob that I knocked about with all used to hang out down the very bottom end of the Wap.

"Mandi and her crew all used to hang about where the table football was.

"I used to see her hanging about but it was years before I ever spoke to her. It used to be absolutely brilliant down there.

"I worked on the Wap door from 1991 until 1993. I was head doorman.

"It was a weird door to work because, fundamentally, everyone coming in there was of a similar mindset. It wasn't like a normal town pub where anything could happen.

"It wasn't a hard door to work at all. We didn't work it trying to be tough guys because, if anything did kick off downstairs, you'd got an army at your back because you knew everybody.

"Hardest part of the job was getting everybody out at the end of the night

because nobody wanted to go.

"I'd love to know how much money I spent on Newcastle Brown in there over the years.

"Steve Stokes, who was head doorman at Rebels, was my best mate for quite a long time. We used to do a lot of rock climbing together. On a lot of occasions, even when they had the all nighters on at Rebels, I'd work on the door of the Wap. When it had finished I'd pick up my rucksack full of gear from behind the bar, trot off to Rebels and stop there until that finished and then we'd be off to North Wales or somewhere climbing. We never bothered with any sleep or anything like that. We were always in a right pickle by the afternoon!

"If there were any big stars playing City Hall we'd often get them in the Wap. Eric Clapton has been in. Mate of mine went in there one night and at one side of him he'd got Jeff Beck and the other side Jimmy Page. I've seen Rob Halford walk in there. Steve Clarke out of Leppard used to go in now and again."

Chapter 3

GLITTER, SAXON AND A FUTURE NWOBHM DRUMMING POWER HOUSE

PETE GILL (SECOND FROM LEFT) WITH GARY GLITTER AND THE GLITTER BAND

Pete Gill was definitely one of the country's most influential and formidable rock drummers of the late seventies and eighties but that's only half his story.

In terms of his ability to criss-cross musical genres and achieve chart success at the very highest level, his success was virtually untouchable in the region and stretched over a staggering three decades.

He was far more than a drummer – he was a great songwriter, arranger and organiser in a rock'n'roll world where debauchery was king.

Pete Gill helped turn rising rock act, Son Of A Bitch, into world-beating, NWOBHM leading Saxon, and help return Motorhead to mainstream success.

He definitely had a very un-metal beginning to his career but it was always a lifelong passion for Led Zeppelin that edged him in the direction of metal.

The powerhouse drummer – whose face would adorn the front cover of rock mags across the globe for the majority of the 1980s – was the token white face in soul band Midnight Express in the sixties before going on to enjoy a formidable career with a trio of chart topping acts: Gary Glitter's Glitter Band, Saxon and Motorhead.

When he wasn't hitting hell out of his skins he was back in Sheffield fishing – a slightly less frenetic passion of his.

Pete Gill said: "I started off playing in local bands and I was studying drumming as well so I rapidly advanced up to a very good level and more and more people asked me to go and play for them.

"I was in a soul band called Midnight Express at the time. We'd got a full brass section and we used to open for Arthur Conley and all the American stars and we did all the big circuit. They were all black and I was just the seventeen year old white boy. It was fantastic – I still see them today.

"My ex-wife's friend's husband was the chief road manager for the Alan Bown Set who were a massive soul band at that time. He was in an organistion that got to work with some big London artists and along the way he met Mike Leander [famed arranger and producer that helped mastermind Glitter's career in the 1970s] .

"Mike Leander said he desperately needed another drummer that could really play for a new band he was working with that was playing with two drummers.

"The guitarist and the bass player ended up coming to see me. At that time they didn't mean anything to

Pete Gill

Pete Gill with Gary Glitter

me as they were only a project and weren't known.

"They told me they were going to hit the charts – usual sort of stuff where you were thinking 'oh yeah, right, fine!'

"As it turned out they asked me to go to a gig they were doing at a big club in Scarborough to talk to the rest of the band and Mike Leander.

"I saw the band play and they were absolutely fantastic.

"They finished the set and the crowd were going absolutely wild for an encore. The tour manager came rushing over and said 'just follow me'. He took me through the crowd and I found out the other drummer had collapsed after the gig.

"He said 'well you're going on' and the other drummer said 'just follow what I play'. I'd no nerves in those days and I just thought 'well bring it on'! It was really funny because Gary Glitter came on and he looked one way and then looked straight at me and did a double-take as I'm just sat there dressed normally whilst the rest of the band are dressed like tarts!

"Straight after the gig the band simply came up to me and said 'will you join?' And that was it.

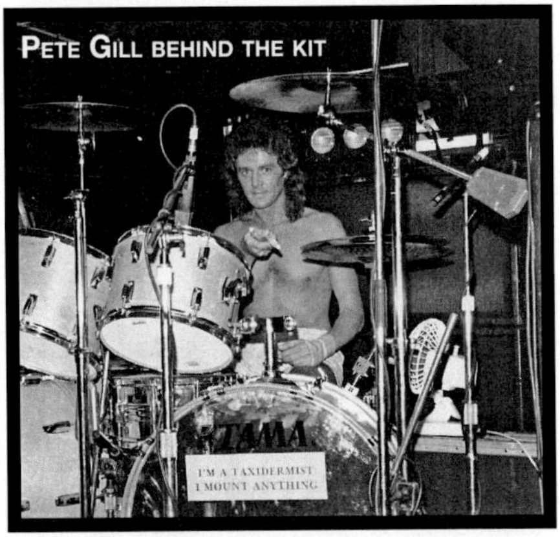

Pete Gill behind the kit

"The reaction to the gigs was unbelievable – we were a really good band. The first two nights I ever played at Sheffield City Hall was with Glitter. I was probably the only person from Sheffield playing in the glam scene at the time.

"In those days, with that sort of band, you needed an escort into the show and out again. I always remember being impressed with the dressing rooms, even though they were the old fashioned dressing rooms and, at that time, people could actually sit behind the stage, so we'd got another 200 or so people behind us, which was very unusual.

"I also liked the security with their dark red blazers – jobsworths, but great. I used to get along with them really well."

Pete Gill said he'd probably have liked to take the band on a sightseeing tour of Sheffield at the time but admitted things would have simply got out of hand.

He said: "Because of the popularity of the band, wherever you went you got mobbed. So if we went in a club you'd never be left alone. VIP areas, in those days, were very few and far between.

"I'd done the second Australian tour with Glitter which was absolutely manic. It got to about the end of 1974 and I sort of re-discovered Led Zeppelin and I decided I'd had enough plus I could see glam rock was beginning to wane in England and other stuff was coming through.

"I ended up doing a favour for a friend of mine and went to help out a covers band in Germany and it was great just to get away. I become a session player over there.

"I came back to England for a long weekend to see Led Zeppelin's 'The Song Remains The Same'.

Pete Gill with Phil 'Filthy Animal' Taylor and (right) with Twisted Sister's Dee Snider

"It hadn't been out very long and I think it was the back end of 1975. I was stopping in a hotel near Earl's Court and when I left one day I saw this vendor selling Melody Maker. I got the paper and saw this big ad for a top band with top lights, top pa etc wanting drummer. It turned out they didn't have anything! That was Son Of A Bitch [later to become Saxon]. And it was really strange because I was planning to come up and see my mother in Sheffield the following day so I arranged to go up and have a blast with the band as well – and the blast lasted three hours because they'd got the energy and the power and so had I. We just gelled and I said I'd join the band. I went back to Germany and sorted everything out there and came straight back and started to play.

"In those days there were big bucks to be made at Working Men's Clubs but the type of music we were playing didn't lend itself to that scene. But in places like Wales, the North East, round Birmingham and places like that there used to be rock nights and they'd be queuing up at six o'clock. There could be four, five or six hundred people all queuing up outside in places like Sunderland and Newcastle.

"Because of the distances it wasn't viable to get back but we also couldn't afford to stay places but we also needed to book four, five or six gigs together whilst we were away. So we ended up buying a big, old van and partitioned that off and had bus seats.We'd play the gig, leave all the gear in the venue, get the sleeping bags out and sleep in the van. Next day we'd get up and get washed, the two crew would get the gear and we'd be off. And we built it up from there. Sometimes we'd hire the room, promote it and have someone on the door collecting the money.

"We actually got signed to Carrere Records, which was a big deal at the time, at the Boilermakers' Club in Sunderland. John Verity from Argent was a good friend of the band and ended up producing our first album. He got the label interested. We played at the Boilermakers' and he brought one of the bigwigs up from the management company in London and they signed us over the phone. We did the first set and this guy from London said 'if we don't fucking sign them someone else will' and that was how it was done.

"We flew over to France the following week. They stumped up the money for the first album and away we sent.

"We only played in Sheffield with Son Of A Bitch once and that was at The Limit.

We got paid up for being too loud. We went on and after, I think, the third number that was it. Think we took about an 8k rig in there, in reality it was probably more like 4 or 5k.

We definitely played like it was an 8k! So Kevan Johnson [the co-owner] came up and said 'no, no, no – we're not having this, I've got customers to think about, now get off!'

"I was always down The Limit. I thought The Limit was probably one of the best clubs I've ever been to vibe and band wise. I saw some amazing bands down there."

Anyone that has ever been in a band knows drummers are regularly proven to be a breed apart. Pete Gill reckons they can't help it.

He said: "I don't know about guitarists but drummers seem to be born with it – they can't keep their hands and feet still.

"My first gig was at Dore & Totley Youth Club [in Sheffield] and I remember we all took the equipment on the bus."

Pete Gill is the first to congratulate fellow Sheffielders Def Leppard on their success: "In America bands like Saxon and Motorhead only have a limited market and there's little crossover whereas Joe Cocker and Def Leppard, especially Def Leppard, have done more for us than anyone. What a fantastic band.

"I can remember them as kids coming to see us at Sheffield City Hall.

"They used to come into The Stonehouse [Sheffield city centre pub] with their leopard skin trousers and sneak in for a quick half and get talking to us and they'd say 'we're going to be as big as you one day' and I'd say 'I hope you are'. And they were – ten times bigger!"

Pete Gill's Saxon and Motorhead tour diary of the eighties reads like a who's who of rock.

He said: "We [Saxon] did a lot of support tours and the first big one we did was with Motorhead which was 42 gigs back to back. That was some going and incredibly successful for them but also successful for us.

"Straight after that we did the Nazareth tour. Our first album hadn't done massive things but we followed that straight up with 'Wheels of Steel' which helped us make the transition from supporting to headlining within a short time. So from supporting for two nights at Sheffield City Hall we were now headlining two nights.

"We were playing with (a), people we really wanted to play with and (b), people we'd worshipped.

SAXON, MOTORHEAD AND CREW

"Our first massive European tour was with Judas Priest and they were absolutely phenomenal but we were up there and we'd already done Donington with them. And we went to America and opened for Rush which was unbelievable because by that time we were getting used to playing two to three thousand seaters but with them we were playing 25,000 to 30,000 seaters every night. That was something else. It was an amazing tour.

"Finished that and went straight on to the Black Sabbath tour. They were playing the same venues and Ronnie James Dio had just joined them. Fantastic. And then we did some dates with AC/DC and Brian had just joined the band. It was funny in that it was the first tour Sabbath had done with Dio and the first tour AC/DC had done with Brian and they were both staggering."

Pete Gill was already enamoured with AC/DC since the first time he caught them at a very early Sheffield gig.

"I saw probably the second UK date AC/DC ever did in England at Lower Refractory, Pond Street, in Sheffield in, I

LED ZEPPELIN'S JIMMY PAGE (SECOND FROM LEFT) WITH MOTORHEAD AND PETE GILL

think, 1977. I was staggered, I'd never seen anything like it. We were powerful, very, but I'd never seen the way they played before. From beginning to end it was like... God almighty!

"Malcolm Young is something to be reckoned with as a rhythm player and Phil Rudd is playing quarter notes, eighths and sixteenths which nobody else did. Most people played beats on the bass drums with the bass player but he didn't. It was absolutely staggering.

"So by the time we met up with them again Bon had died, Brian had joined and they were fantastic.

"We did Top Of The Pops with Brian in 1973 when he was with Geordie. I'd not seen him since then so we had a good chinwag. AC/DC were fantastic to us. So were Rush. So were Judas Priest. Never had a problem. Didn't have much to do with Black Sabbath. Not because there was anything wrong. Because it was a new tour and they'd got lots of stage production stuff they wanted to get right.

"I was fired for an unsavoury reason on Saxon's behalf. I was offered a few things in-between which I wasn't really interested but then I got a call one day from Motorhead's manager.

"The band's management sent me eight songs to listen to, which I did, and they weren't a problem to learn. I went down to London and everything was set up, I played, and that was it."

The Motorhead camp were more than impressed but Pete Gill wasn't to be rushed.

"Lemmy said 'please join' and I said I'd think about it", he admits.

Pete Gill, quite rightly, wanted to be far more than a hired hand. His perseverance paid off and his influence was felt from day one.

His inauguration was immediately followed by the release of double compilation album, 'No Remorse', including the new 'Killed By Death' co-written by Pete Gill, twenty of the band's classics and another three new tracks.

Their next album, 'Orgasmatron', reached new levels in fury – much of it orchestrated by Pete Gill's armageddon-like backline. It succeeded in getting the band back on track to commercial success.

The album reached No 21 in the album charts.

Pete Gill said: "The production on 'Orgasmatron' was staggering, David

MOTORHEAD ON THEIR TRAVELS

Bowie's producer did it.

"When he came down to see us in pre-production I don't think he took it all in. He was used to things with Bowie like 'Lets Dance' with incredible drum sound. He'd never been hit with a wall like that. In the room that he came to see us we played as loud as we did on stage. And bless him, he just stood there nodding and he must have been thinking 'Jesus Christ Almighty!!!' as we were blowing him against the wall.

"He did a fantastic job on the album and on 'Orgasmatron' there are lots of limiters and gates and big drum sounds where I really had to whack the kit to get the best out of it.

"But unfortunately we had to go straight back to America after that album and we didn't get to mix it."

Lemmy's total lack of any type of time schedule, according to Pete Gill, was the last straw as far as drumming for Motorhead was concerned.

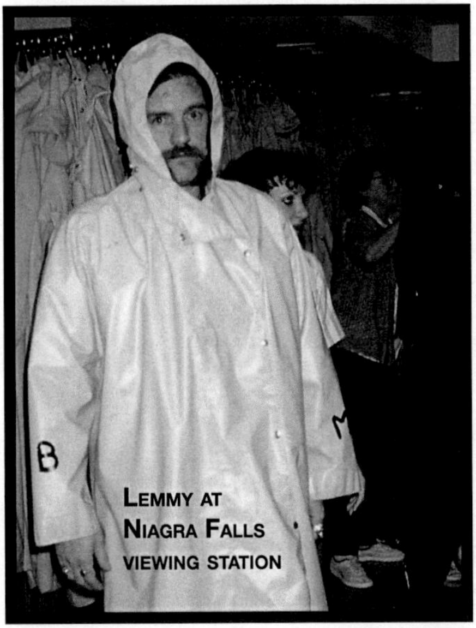
LEMMY AT NIAGRA FALLS VIEWING STATION

Pete Gill said: "I ended up having a massive fall out with Lemmy and that was it, I just walked away. Something happened that day, it broke my spirit. I gave my all. I nearly died every night on stage for that. I don't like letting people down and he'd let people down quite a few times. On this occasion it was just once too many. We'd got a film crew waiting to do 'The Young Ones', that's where it all came from."

He admits his debut performing at the UK's biggest rock festival with Saxon was one of his career highs.

He said: "First time at Donington's Monsters of Rock was a milestone in this country because they'd not had anything like that before. It was a fantastic bill. You came out the dressing room and everyone's stood around like Rainbow, Judas Priest and Scorpions.

"We came out having been championed in the music press by Geoff Barton and it was like, watch this... We went on and that did it for us. That was a real turning point.

"There've been so many highs and lows in my career. Meeting absolute idols like Neil Peart and getting friendly with him. It was their thing that they never really spoke to anyone. They're not horrible people, they're fantastic, they do things before they go on stage

"Neil Peart took me in Alex's dressing room and he builds model aeroplanes. He's stood there, before he goes on stage in front of 25,000 people, painting and putting glue on. I found that hard to understand because, before a gig, we'd be pacing up and down with ZZ Top blaring out of the cassette player.

"And what afforded me the greatest honour of all time was meeting Jimmy Page. We used to rehearse in Nomis Studio in London which is a massive complex so at any one time you'd have us, Duran Duran, Spandau Ballet, Emerson Lake and Palmer, Culture Club and loads of others. At this particular time we were down for three weeks and Jimmy Page was next door with a band called The Firm. Once I'd seen 'The Song Remains The Same' I thought nobody's going to follow that. I don't think anybody has his charisma. Well it blew me away because we were having 15 minutes break and so were they. He walked into our rehearsal room and Lemmy said 'this is Pete, this is Jim'. And I thought, it's Jimmy Page – I hadn't recognised him! But we got chatting and I ensured I didn't ask him anything about Jon Bonham because I was a big Jon Bonham freak... Still am.

"But Jimmy was asking our guitarist, Phil Campbell, about his Les Paul.

PETE GILL (LEFT) HAS THE SENSE TO LEAVE THE SPEEDOS IN THE HOTEL ROOM

Jimmy picked it up and played and said 'that's really fantastic – do you mind if I play it for a couple of days, I'll lend you mine?'

"He picked the guitar up and played all the intro for 'Stairway To Heaven' with me and Phil. I thought that'll do for me. I'll never have to see or do anything again!"

Barnsley's Saxon, complete with Sheffield drummer Pete Gill, "taught America how to head bang".

Originally entitled Son Of A Bitch, the original line-up was completed by Biff Byford (vocals), Paul Quinn (guitar), Graham Oliver (guitar) and Steve Dawson (bass).

They formed in 1979 and successfully tempted Pete Gill back from a stint in Germany following his time drumming with Gary Glitter and the Glitter Band.

Subtlety was never a by-word for the Saxon school of metal. Picked up by Carrere Records, their self-titled debut album offered tunes such as 'Stallions Of The Highway' and 'Big Teaser'.

But though their spandex-wearing, testosterone attitude with a dash of the axe-wielding Middle Ages was always going to give rise to a love them or hate them attitude, they possessed the ability to pen some mighty metal anthems that became a call to arms the world over in the eighties.

In fact their success was pretty staggering. They happily joined up as one of the key exponents of the British New Wave of Heavy Metal movement and whilst Iron Maiden came with mascot Eddie, Motorhead had a lighting gantry inspired by their 'Bomber' album, Saxon came with their own giant eagle shaped one, dubbed Biff's budgie by the road crew apparently.

Their 1980 album, 'Wheels of Steel', was massive and closely followed by 'Strong Arm Of The Law' in the same year.

SAXON BACKSTAGE WITH MEMBERS OF SUPPORT BAND LIMELIGHT

Chris Twiby said: "1980 was an iconic year for metal if ever there was one with AC/DC and Priest selling millions. Saxon played the first ever Donington and went down a storm. My mate had spoken to Biff on various occasions before but on that day, when he bumped into the front man who sported the tightest silver satin trousers you have ever seen, with a young lady on his arm, he was snubbed. This went down very badly. Biff had obviously got too big for his loyal fans. My mate wasn't happy but had to admit they were very good onstage."

Top Of The Pops, Monsters of Rock Festival and every rock'n'roll trapping followed as the frenetic Saxon train rolled forward culminating in 'The Eagle Has Landed' live album in 1982.

Drummer Pete Gill had already gone following a hand injury and wasn't around to witness the softening of the Saxon sound to try and win over America and MTV.

The hits dried up but the band carried on regardless. Even the onset of 1990s grunge and its purge on metal couldn't stop South Yorkshire's finest.

Saxon's Graham Oliver, Biff Byford and Steve Dawson

Pete Gill (left), Biff Byford (second from right) with Saxon's Japanese tour manager and their manager David Poxon (right)

The band (or you could say two bands – there's also an 'Oliver/Dawson Saxon' these days) have enjoyed a bit of a resurgence in recent years following Saxon's appearance (this was the Biff Byford version) on a Channel 4 reality TV show which saw promoter Harvey Goldsmith giving the band a few home truths on how to revive their fortunes.

Hundreds also attended a gig by Oliver/Dawson Saxon at Sheffield's Midland Railway Station in 2009.

Pete Gill's last outing with former members of Saxon was actually at the Midland Hotel in Killamarsh, Sheffield, for the 50th birthday of Dez Bailey of The Bailey Brothers.

He was joined on stage by Graham Oliver, Steve Dawson and Dez Bailey.

Pete generally enjoys a quieter life these days – his musical legacy more than assured.

Steve Dawson boasts a legacy of a different kind. He is cited as the inspiration for bassist Derek Smalls in mock rock documentary 'This Is Spinal Tap'.

Punk leanings of the natural born NWOBHM leaders

No rock musician was more aware of the rise and influence of punk than future Saxon guitarist Graham Oliver.

He was gigging with Steve Dawson – future Saxon bassist – from the early 1970s under the name Sob, named after Free album 'Tons of Sob'.

Graham Oliver said of the fledgling punk bands: "Although some of the punk bands were really good I think some just hid behind the fashion. You could get away with that in London but in Sheffield or Leeds you couldn't. You had to be able to back up what you were supposed to stand for on a live performance otherwise you'd just get bottled.

"We were brought up on all that stuff. We had the energy and respect and were doing gigs with the Heavy Metal Kids [fronted by Gary Holton who sang for The Damned for a short while] and they were pretty much crossover. One of our very first gigs with Pete Gill was supporting The Clash at Belle Vue in Manchester. We ended up doing it a couple of times.

"I remember the night Marc Bolan died – we were playing with the Heavy Metal Kids in Cardiff and Marc Bolan was just getting into being friends with punk bands.

"When we signed our record deal we were rubbing shoulders with people like Rat Scabies [drummer of The Damned]."

It was actually the onset of punk that persuaded them to change their name from Sob to something a little more anarchic to fit with the changing times.

Graham Oliver said: "Alan Bown [of the Alan Bown Set] came and introduced himself and said 'I'm from Sheffield and I used to have a band called the Alan Bown Set. We'd now got Biff [Byford] with us but we'd been booked under Sob but the gig had been booked before Biff and Paul Quinn actually joined us. Alan said 'because of all this punk going off Sob's too naff. You ought to be angry young men. You should change it to Son Of A Bitch'. So we did. It was only about four years later that we got a record deal. When Carrerre Records wanted a licensing deal in 1979, just prior to our first album being released, people in America said 'no way – you can't be Son Of A Bitch, it's just not going to happen.'

"So we had to change the name to Saxon which was a lengthy process and we went through loads of names."

Though Saxon have always been hailed as "Barnsley's finest" they had more in common with Sheffield argues Graham Oliver, and that's even before they started with Sheffield's own Pete Gill.

"It was Biff and Quinny that were from Barnsley", he explains. "Me and Steve were always in the Sheffield pubs. We'd catch the train from Mexborough to Sheffield and walk down The Moor and walk all the way up London Road to the music shops and then to Berkeley Precinct to Johnson Electrics to look at Fender Stratocasters.

"Me and Steve cut our teeth in Sheffield at The Black Swan going to see Patto and Status Quo when they were trying to re-invent themselves as a twelve-bar band. Every Sunday night, for twelve bob, was The Black Swan rock night.

"We used to practice in The Albert which was sited straight across the road from Sheffield City Hall. At the venues they'd be having Deep Purple, Black Sabbath and all these bands. We'd start practising at 7.30 or 8 o'clock and when it got to about ten past ten we'd see a few people had started leaving to catch buses and things. That was our cue to down instruments, dash across the road and get straight in to the back of Sheffield City Hall because security had all gone to the front and there was nobody on the door. We got to see all the bands free like Deep Purple and Led Zeppelin – it was unbelievable. "

Though it might not always have been planned, Saxon were far more of a punk/metal crossover band than people give them credit and couldn't have been better equipped to lead the NWOBHM charge.

Graham Oliver said: "We went down well with punk audiences – we'd got the energy. People were rarely hostile even though we looked different. We were very much influenced by the energy that the punks had and we'd go for it hammer and tongs.

"If you listen to our live Donington album you can hear how it's kicking and fast.

"I remember cutting my hand on one of Gilly's cymbals after he kicked it over. I kept on playing and there was blood all over my white Gibson SG, blood spattered all over my face and these kids were going 'it's brilliant, it's just like watching The Clash' – they were loving it. It was more by accident than design but all that stuff helped.

"We weren't like your archetypal ten minute guitar solos or anything like that. We were pretty wild. We'd got the energy, the musicianship and the fast-paced songs like 'Heavy Metal Thunder' and 'Motorcycle Man'. We ended up doing Top Of The Pops with Johnny Rotten – he was doing 'Flowers of Romance'.

The Saxon line-up that stormed Donington's first Monsters of Rock and took them to the top of their game is still regarded as the best by many in the business. Graham agrees but with hindsight he thinks it was too much, too soon, and didn't help their long-game.

Graham Oliver said: "Pete Gill is definitely the best Saxon drummer of all time and even Lars Ulrich, this year, told me that. He was totally innovative and challenging and he really pushed us. Everything fell into place when he joined.

"First time we rehearsed with him it was at Mexborough Grammar School.

"It was like a rollercoaster at that point. The NWOBHM took off and everyone was tipping Def Leppard to be the big one and we ended up out-selling them and Iron Maiden. In hindsight I wish it would have been the other way around because we had our decline quicker. The Darkness is a classic example. When you get that big, that fast it sometimes can't sustain itself. Leppard did it a bit more gradual.

"I remember playing Sheffield City Hall and all Leppard were stood at the side of the stage watching us."

Chapter 4

We fought The States and we won - Def Leppard

Nothing has ever nailed Sheffield's rock credentials to the global map like Def Leppard.

With over three decades at the top of their game, they remain one of the biggest acts of their generation and even returned to headline Donington's Download festival in 2009, nearly a quarter of a century since they last played the hallowed site of metaldom in 1986.

Though their highly polished sound hasn't always been to everyone's liking in the UK, it was just the ticket for America who turned them into a multi-platinum selling, stadium-busting money making machine of gargantuan proportions.

The roots of the band can be traced right back to the mid-1970s when 15-year-old Rick Savage swallowed his pride – he was, and continues to be, a SWFC fan – and signed up for SUFC.

His footballing career didn't last.

He soon got disillusioned and decided to form a band with friend Tony Kenning.

Rick Savage promptly ordered a electric guitar from his mother's catalogue.

Rehearsals began at Tapton Youth Club under the moniker 'Atomic Mass'.

Their short career ended with a gig at Tapton School gym playing rock covers. The band also comprised future Def Leppard member Pete Willis on guitar together with Nicholas McKay on vocals and guitarist Paul Hampshire.

But fate, they soon learned, was just yards away from them that day. Standing in the audience was one 16-year-old Joe Elliott who'd already started designing posters for his own future band, Deaf Leopard (the lack of any other musicians hadn't been an issue at that point).

He auditioned and got the job for the band.

Joe Elliott's influence was felt almost immediately and the band was relaunched as Def Leppard (the 'Def' came from the deliberate misspelling of 'Led' in Led Zeppelin).

By November 1977 they were practising hard in a rundown spoon factory in the towering Stag Works just a few feet away from the SUFC ground at Bramall Lane. Rick Savage was obviously cursed. Joe Elliott was, and continues to be, SUFC through and through.

Joe Elliott's influence was felt almost immediately and the band was relaunced as Def Leppard

Whilst the rest of the country had spent the last year getting their hair cut, sticking safety pins through their nose and getting hit records via three chords, no guitar solos and general anti-hero bravado the Leppard boys were working tirelessly to grow their hair, master the skulduggery of heavy metal guitar pouting wizardry and generally gear themselves up to fly in the face of anything remotely in vogue at the time.

Steve Clark was added to the line-up after the decision was made that another six string was required to emulate the sound of Thin Lizzy's trademark dual-guitar attack.

They were soon rehearsing four nights a week and all day Sunday without even playing a gig.

Their first 'official' gig took place on July 18, 1978, at Westfield School in Sheffield.

The gig, as is the case with just about every debut gig in the history of the Western World, didn't get off to the best of starts.

Joe Elliott: "Just as we were about to go on, we realised we hadn't tuned the guitars. So we had to get one of the guys helping us to bring Steve's Marshall amp into the dressing room. We tuned up on that. But when it was set up again on stage, the switch was left on standby. Steve plugged in and walked to the front of the stage, looking the part in his tight jeans and long blond hair. He was all ready to go into the first song, 'World Beyond The Sky', he did his windmill arm motion, just like Pete Townshend, for the big opening chord – and nothing happened. No power. Everybody in the audience was laughing. After a few seconds, we started all over again."

Sept 11, 1978 was one of the more bizarre line-ups in Sheffield's musical history and definitely Def Leppard's.

It was the one and only time the future multi-million album-selling rock monsters would support rising Sheffield electro-stars Human League in day one of a two-day free local music festival at West Street's legendary Limit club.

Graph, Ton Trick and/or Monitors (nobody seems quite sure which of these two acts actually played) were sandwiched between the two acts that went on to global domination. (Day two of the soiree didn't produce any more Sheffield music legends unfortunately.)

Garry Wilson, Artery drummer who once failed a Def Leppard audition through an inability to know 'Stairway to Heaven' and went on to be the manager of The Limit, said: "George Webster [the venue's co-owner], in his infinite wisdom, booked Def Leppard on the same bill as Human League. The League turned up with all these synthesisers or whatever and then produced all these Perspex screens which they then put round the synths. I asked what they were for and they said they were expecting trouble that night. Sure enough, because it was a rock audience, the glasses starting flying at them."

The Human League were already used to a hostile reaction in some quarters: they'd even considered crash helmets at one point.

A previous gig supporting punk act The Rezillos (which included future Human League member Jo Callis in the line-up) in London had prompted band member Ian Marsh to put together a greenhouse-resembling bunch of Perspex screens to protect his synthesizer from flying missiles for the first time.

The Limit show was only Def Leppard's third proper gig.

Human League front man Phil Oakey was quite inspired by the fledgling Leppard.

"Def Leppard were pretty obviously serious from the start. Of all the bands around I think they were the ones that knew exactly what they were doing. I was never dismissive of them."

LIMIT FLYER FOR THE ONE AND ONLY TIME DEF LEPPARD SUPPORTED HUMAN LEAGUE

DEF LEPPARD'S ORIGINAL MANAGER PETE MARTIN (SECOND LEFT) OUTSIDE THE REVOLUTION SHOP ON CASTLE MARKET WITH PAUL WELLER (SECOND FROM RIGHT)

Limit owners George Webster and Kevan Johnson were quite happy with Def Leppard because they already had a strong following, which meant plenty of cash over the bar.

Def Leppard bassist Rick Savage remembers the outing well. The whole band ended up becoming regulars at the club.

"The Limit more or less coincided with our band starting out. I was seventeen and I was just about old enough to go and drink in bars.

"My first experience of going in there was when there was a free concert for all local bands that George Webster and Kevan Johnson had put on – there were around ten bands on.

"We were the only heavy metal band on the bill – it wasn't the time for hard rock as it was right at the top of the punk era or it was more art-schooly. People would laugh if you were starting a hard rock band.

"I remember thinking 'how can they [Human League] be any good, they've not even got a drummer'. Little did we know that years later we'd go down the same route with sequencing and bringing that into the hard rock genre.

"We went down a storm because most of the audience were our friends and it was an open house [free to get in]. We kind of stole the show for that reason and Kevan and George immediately said 'we'll book you'. We came back and headlined.

"The week before we headlined Kevan barred Steve Clarke, our guitarist, and another of us. There was an altercation in the club, everyone had had too much to drink, and Steve – god love him – stood out and he got thrown up the stairs.

"He shouted: 'You can't bar me I'm playing here next week.' So they let him back in!

"Once you'd played there you got to know George and Kevan and it became a nice place to go and we genuinely

The band perform at Virgin on Fargate

liked it. It was cheap beer and after hours and there were the old arcade games, like Pac Man, there. We'd go every Friday night regularly.

"It was hard rock and punk and everything in between. It was a really cool place to hang out.

"I think there were a few question marks around the first time we played down there. We ended up with about 800 people in there and walked out with £50! And we thought, 'hang on a minute – something's not right here'.

"The dressing room was more like an overgrown wardrobe but that was part of the vibe of the place. It was crap but it was all part of the charm.

"The dressing room was more like an overgrown wardrobe"
Rick Savage

"When you look back you've got to be thankful for a place like The Limit. We didn't want to go down the route of playing Working Men's Clubs. It gave bands like us a chance and punters a chance to see new bands."

Chris Westwood reviewed the band's first Limit gig for Record Mirror. The slating helped in a way; it named the band's own record label.

He said: "Def Leppard were heavy metal as heavy metal always was and will always be. Crosses, macho poses, bludgeon riffola that even the Sabs (Black Sabbath) abandoned years ago, and ironically, we thought the only band to screw the audience for an encore."

The band's Bludgeon Riffola label released the Def Leppard EP in January 1979. These days it's worth a small fortune...

Another very early and celebrated gig took place at the city's Wapentake Bar.

John Alflat: "Def Leppard approached the manager, Olga Marshall, about doing a gig there. She was initially worried about the age of some of the band as I believe either one or two of them were under the legal drinking age. They agreed to be paid a fee of £15.

"They set up in the early evening: no effects, no light show just the basic band set up. There was a reasonable crowd in as the band had already built a following.

"The one striking thing I remember was the attitude of singer Joe Elliott. He was a powerful and confident singer even then and didn't appear to have any nerves."

The band set out their stall for greatness very early in their careers. It's no surprise they needed the States to fulfil their ambitions.

Joe Elliott said: "We always wanted to be the biggest band in the world. Our yardstick when we started was the Stones and Zeppelin and The Who and The Beatles, which may have seemed like a foolish dream at the time."

Indie music die hard John Peel, rather surprisingly, was the first national DJ to give the band airplay. Colin Slade of Radio Hallam in Sheffield was the first DJ to air their song.

Fellow Radio Hallam DJ, Dave Kilner, was also a key supporter of the band throughout his life.

Def Leppard initially found management in the shape of Pete Martin, owner of legendary Revolution Records that stood not far away from The Penthouse nightclub (which later became Rebels) on Castle Market in Sheffield with Arista Records plugger Frank Stuart-Brown.

News of the band reached two of the most influential media people in the UK's rock world at that point – Geoff Barton of Sounds and photographer Ross Halfin.

They headed north to see the band in June 1979 which led to a three-page spread in the national music press.

A BBC Radio One session followed in its wake and by August they'd been snapped up by Phonogram.

The record deal had to be completed at drummer Rick Allen's house because he was underage and his father had to sign on his behalf.

THE AFTERMATH OF RICK ALLEN'S DEVASTATING CAR CRASH ON NEW YEAR'S EVE 1984 THAT SEVERED HIS LEFT ARM. MASSIVELY TRAUMATISED, BUT UNBOWED, THE DRUMMER VOWED TO PLAY AGAIN

RICK ALLEN IN HIS CUSTOMISED ELECTRONIC KIT ALLOWING DRUM EFFECTS TO BE TRIGGERED VIA PEDALS

Few school leavers celebrate their sixteenth birthday in such spectacular and enviable fashion as Rick Allen either – he spent it on stage at Hammersmith Odeon supporting AC/DC!

Def Leppard were also caught by AC/DC's tour manager Peter Mensch who went on to be their manager and help them to become one of the biggest bands in the world.

Despite incredible success tragedy has never been far from the door of the band.

On New Year's Eve, 1984, 21-year-old Rick Allen, riding high on Pyromania selling six million albums in the States (with a measly comparable sales of just 30,000 in the UK), crashed his new Chevrolet Corvette Stingray on the A57 near Sheffield.

He lost his left arm and it looked like his drumming career was at an end.

Rick Allen's subsequent comeback became one of the biggest stories of the music world in the eighties via a customised kit and his own willpower.

Pete Willis was replaced by former Girl guitarist Phil Collen a year earlier. Drink was blamed for getting in the way of the band's progress.

Sales of their next album, Hysteria, which went on to top a staggering 15 million, made them the biggest and most successful act to ever come out of Sheffield.

Tragedy struck once again in January 1991 with the death of guitarist Steve Clark. He was found dead at his Chelsea flat after a drinking binge. He overdosed on a mixture of alcohol, painkillers and anti-depressants.

The band had kept a lid on his alcoholism for a long time. He was replaced by Irish guitarist Vivian Campbell. Phil Collen's former band mate, Girl guitarist Gerry Laffy, was hotly tipped for the job at the time.

Gerry Laffy said: "'Phil Collen called me to say he wanted me to join the band, I was flattered but sceptical, he asked me to learn four or five songs and fly to LA to rehearse with the band and see how it played out, he really wanted me to join him, but Joe had a mate, Vivian Campbell, who he was championing. I had just signed a new five year management contract with Russell Mulcahy, so I decided that I wasn't gonna go to LA so it became a one man race.

"From my point of view Vivian was the better choice. Phil and I are still pals 30 years after we first met, there was no hard feelings, it was just the way things panned out."

Def Leppard survived the advent of grunge that was the death knell for scores of eighties hair rock bands and, even though they seem to have a bit of a shaky start to the 21st century, their latest album, 'Songs From The Sparkle Lounge', has seen a massive return to form and commercial success.

Recent gigs have seen them at their most happening and hungriest in years.

There have been so many high points in the career

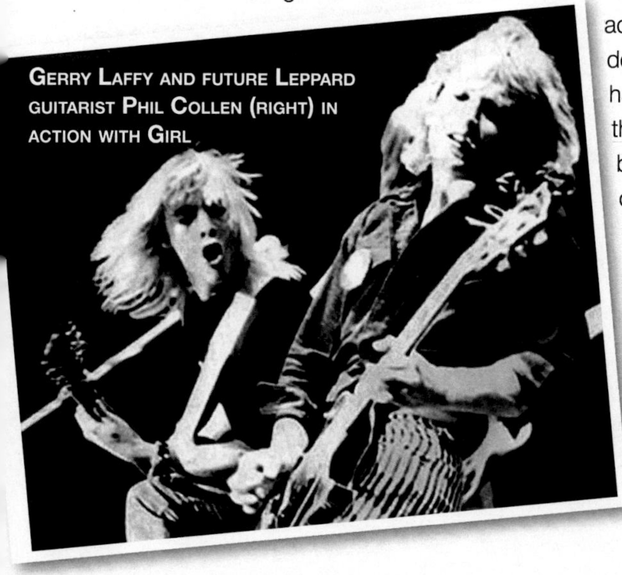

GERRY LAFFY AND FUTURE LEPPARD GUITARIST PHIL COLLEN (RIGHT) IN ACTION WITH GIRL

of Def Leppard but some of the most notable have been the ones bestowed on them by their home city.

The 1995 Def Leppard Day must be one of the most poignant as the world's music press descended on Sheffield.

The event was such a milestone it even persuaded titles like the NME – hardly a publication noted for its gushing reports on the band – to swallow its pride and high-tail up the M1 to Steel City.

Early planning didn't all go that brilliantly.

The author of this book, who co-ordinated much of the day, was tasked with booking a 'back to their roots' style gig at Sheffield's Wapentake Bar, scene of some of earliest and most memorable gigs.

It was going to be quite a coup for a cellar bar with a capacity of a couple of hundred to book a 'secret' gig by a band that had just become the first band to headline and sell out Sheffield's Don Valley Stadium and had spent nigh on the last 15 years on stadium tours of the USA.

A feat only matched in subsequent years by the likes of Rolling Stones, U2, Red Hot Chilli Peppers and a couple more.

The member of staff on duty at the Wapentake Bar that night didn't see it as a coup one bit.

"Sorry love, we don't put bands on anymore", she exclaimed.

A few things were explained to her by Wapentake Bar matriarch, Olga Marshall, when she got wind of things the following day.

One slight hiccup later and Def Leppard were duly booked for their first Wapentake gig in years and the press began booking their hotel rooms in Sheffield.

The hastily arranged Def Leppard Day HQ phone rang round-the-clock from that day onwards as fans, family members, hangers on and every other Tom, Dick and Harry related to the band did their utmost to land one of the hottest tickets in the history of Sheffield rock.

THE PASS FOR THE BAND'S LEGENDARY RETURN MATCH AT WAPENTAKE BAR

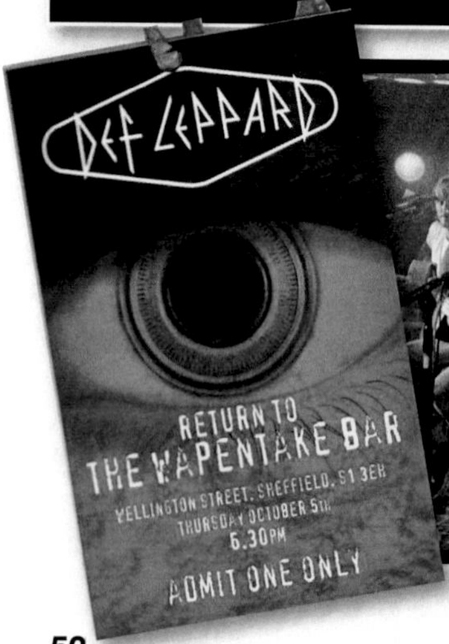

DEF LEPPARD RETURN TO THE WAPENTAKE BAR

SIGNIING THE TOWN HALL'S VISITOR BOOK AS PART OF SHEFFIELD'S DEF LEPPARD DAY

Things started in semi-quiet mode as the band headed into the Sheffield suburbs to unveil a plaque in the somewhat unlikely venue that hosted some of their earliest gigs, Crookes Working Men's Club.

Fair enough, they were mobbed when they got in but it was quiet until they opened the door...

They, like the rest of the city, were still under the illusion that the city's planned National Centre for Popular Music was going to have a passing nod to the musical icons that had come from the city (and been more than a little help in justifying the fact it was going to be in Sheffield rather than London).

Anyway, the band donated a guitar as one of the first exhibits for the ill-fated visitor attraction with a nice photo call on the site of the structure which was still set to be built at that point.

The most bizarre event of the day was probably the band's acceptance of tea and cakes with the Lord Mayor in his resplendent parlour in the Town Hall.

Def Leppard were as polite as you like. Maybe one of them will make Sheffield Lord Mayor when their guitars are finally hung up for good.

The band ducked and dived the legions of fans trying to suss out their next move – in this case they wandered through the bowels of Sheffield Town Hall to emerge from a little known tunnel leading straight into the public square without bumping into anyone bar a few bemused security guards.

They then let hundreds of balloons into the sky in Tudor Square at a Hallam FM Roadshow MC-d by a man that championed them from their early days, DJ Dave Kilner who sadly passed away last year.

The final job before picking up their instruments was unveiling a plaque to mark their last homecoming, being the first act to play and sell out Don Valley Stadium.

Their arrival on the knee high stage at the Wapentake Bar was greeted with absolute adulation.

'Up close and personal' covers a multitude of sins but this gig was truly was the essence of the saying. The audience couldn't have been closer if they'd had sat next to Joe Elliott on his stool.

The bar was free and the laminate passes from that memorable evening are probably on eBay for hundreds of pounds.

John Alflat said: "I found out the week before the gig they were coming. Olga was very excited. I got down during the afternoon to watch them finish setting up. Outside the Wapentake there were two hugh artics making the 'secret' gig rather unsecret. Inside, the place was packed with equipment and roadies – I'd never seen so much stuff in the place!

"It was brilliant to see them back and return to their roots. It made Olga's day/week/month/year and they kindly sent her a special framed and autographed picture which they'd had taken with her."

The night finished at a rammed after show party in the bar in the Grosvenor House Hotel in Charter Square.

Def Leppard have never lost touch with their home city. They've turned the Christmas lights on, got their own plaque in the city's walk of fame outside Sheffield Town Hall and played secret gigs in local record shops as well as regular appearances at Sheffield Arena.

Their connections with Girl also continue to this day. The band's former bassist Simon Laffy, brother of Gerry Laffy, plays in Phil Collen's side project Manraze with Sex Pistols drummer Paul Cook.

They also performed at Download in 2009.

THE BAND LINE UP TO SWITCH ON SHEFFIELD'S CHRISTMAS LIGHTS

JOE ELLIOTT

Andy Smith, Def Leppard's first road crew member and lifelong friend of Joe and the band, said: "Elliott & I went to King Teds together. He was a year younger than me and we played football together. He knew people I knew, we used to kick a ball about anywhere around Crookes and Broomhill.

"Favourite place we used to play, believe it or not, was on top of what was then the International supermarket at Broomhill, next to the Nat West bank. We used to love kicking a ball about up there.

"I left school in '74 and obviously Joe being a year younger, we just lost contact. And then one of those quite fortuitous things happened - I was doing a course in business studies and office management at the now defunct Stannington College and I was stood in a dinner queue singing to myself - an old Mott The Hoople song called 'Driving Sister', just one of many people with a tray waiting to get food, and I see Joe. We'd not seen each other for a few years. He's very familiar with Mott's work and we just got talking... old friends.

"Poor old Joe, being that little bit younger than us and probably having more sensible parents, wasn't allowed to go to all the gigs that we would go to. His mum and dad were great people and started letting him go with us eventually and we started just hanging around together. I lived at Crosspool so it was an easy walk down Lydgate Lane for me to meet him.

"We would travel anywhere to see the Doctors Of Madness. We saw Steve Harley and Cockney Rebel. We'd see anybody who played at Sheffield City Hall because it was so easily accessible. Ticket prices would be 70 or 80 pence or maybe a quid. I recall that one time some friends and I refused to go and see Gary Glitter because they were charging £1.20 and we thought that was extortionate.

"After we finished our college course, I went my way but we still kept in touch. One day he said 'I'm in this band' and I said 'That's interesting. What is it?' And he's like 'I'm going to be doing some singing'.

"At that time I knew a woman who was a lorry driver working at the same company as myself, Wigfalls, and she was in a band. We became friends because we were both heavily into rock. She had said 'You don't know a drummer do you?' I didn't but I mentioned it to Joe.

"I passed over Ruth's phone

details and so he went down to a few rehearsals. The band was called Jump. They were doing things like Stranglers covers but it didn't work out because the drummer came back and he expected, wrongly in my opinion, to jump straight back on to his drum stool.

"So poor old Joe missed out on that, but Def Leppard were always destined to happen. The practice rooms down at the old Spoon factory were freezing, numbingly cold, but the rehearsals were fantastic. Just had that hint of professionalism. More than enthusiasm. They were down there far more often than you would imagine teenage kids would be.

"That's what happened with Tony, the first drummer. He had girlfriend problems and missed a golden opportunity. He was a marvellous drummer. He fitted in great with the rest of the guys but he made the wrong choice unfortunately, bless him.

"It's only my opinion but the reason that they did make it was they went for the very sensible route of playing harmonic rock music rather than what is traditionally known as heavy metal. Pete Willis and Steve Clark were a great pairing. They both knew enough about melody, you know, going back to the Thin Lizzy twin guitar days. A good song is a good song if it is something that people can both sing along to and bop up and down to as well. I suppose if they had gone the Black Sabbath route they might still have been successful, I just don't think so.

"I roadied for them from day one basically, and the first gig was at Westfield School. When I say roadied that was me basically asking my dad if I could borrow the car because we needed to get all the equipment out and about. The car was an ex Wigfalls Hillman Avenger Estate. Loads of room in the back for the gear. But everybody helped out, and it goes back to what I was saying about having a good supporting cast, good mates. There were loads of people who helped out and it paid off for the Lepps and they reaped all the rewards, which was fantastic.

"One of the early gigs I specifically remember is a great Christmas gig at the Broadfield pub. It was packed. They did a rock version of White Christmas - they Thin Lizzied White Christmas.

"It is like bottling charisma isn't it? They just had something that a lot of the bands around at the time did not have. Maybe it was their youth, their songs, they weren't particularly bad looking lads so they got a good female following. They were accessible because they were all Sheffield lads, they were great to get on with. They were marvellous company.

"I used to be in a position to get a staff discount to hire a van so that was a bonus. I would hire a Bedford Luton, we'd get all the equipment in, drive up to somewhere like Newcastle, do the gig, drive back through the night and if I got the van back before a certain time we got it a lot cheaper. So everything worked out. But they were hard days to do. Work all day, travel up to Newcastle, help the guys set up the equipment, drive back after the gig and probably get about four hours sleep and then go to work. I didn't mind doing it because they were friends.

"I went with them on the first tour in the 1980s and that was a complete blur but a great experience. I was there on Top Of The Pops when they did 'Hello America' and that was quite exciting because I had never been in the BBC building before. I saw people like Nick Lowe and Elvis Costello wandering the corridors. The Vapors were doing 'Turning Japanese' and Squeeze mimed along to 'Nail In My Heart'. With TOTP, everybody either wanted to be on it or avoided it like the plague. Either way ..... but when you grow up watching Top Of The Pops when it was in its heyday in the early 1970s - it was quite exciting.

"They played in The Penthouse. That was a bastard. Back breaking, lugging gear up all those stairs and there was never enough air in that place. Even as a paying punter you would always be gagging for air. Not exactly the best design. But I loved The Penthouse, it was a great venue.

"The problem with England is also the best thing about England. A brilliant genre-defining band like The Smiths can get massive but I am not overly convinced that somebody like The Smiths would make it in America for instance. Because they were probably too English. Whereas Def Leppard had a transatlantic appeal. They always get a lot of flak, the Leppards, for going to America or 'selling out'. Not my words. It's all bollocks. An album gets released in America, an album get released in Britain.

"It's up to the radio stations who decide whether to play it - if they are not going to play it what can you do? And you have got to look at the support network. If your manager isn't advertising your product...

"They have got some cracking material. They have got an absolutely amazing back catalogue which I still play. I have no hesitation of going down my CD shelf and grabbing a Leppard CD and putting it on. I still think Leppard stuff is fantastic radio music. 'Slang' is one of the finest albums ever made by ANY British band.

"I missed the big one at Don Valley Stadium. I asked when they were playing, booked my holidays and then they changed the date so I missed it!

"We were lucky with the Top Rank. I saw The Clash on the 'Give 'em Enough Rope' tour, The Jam on the 'All Mod Cons' tour, I saw The Adverts at the University – at what was the Poly then, later the Nelson Mandela Building – fantastic. I used to love the punk bands. I am on the cover of a Stranglers single, 'Something Better Change'. The back of my head anyway!

"The Leppards once did a free festival in a field and it got that dark that people had to drive their cars up with their headlights on, shine them on the band as stage lighting. Of course the police came round and shut everything down and poor old Pete Martin's band who was going on last as the headline act, they couldn't play because the police stopped them."

Reg Cliff, DJ at Top Rank (which later became Roxy), said: "Sometime in late '77 I was with friends at Dial House Social Club to watch Bitter Suite play. Before they came on stage a couple of youngsters, recognising me as the DJ from 'Improvision' [the venue's influential Sunday night event that had early gigs by everyone from AC/DC to Judas Priest], came over and started to tell me about the heavy rock band they'd recently formed. They told me who their influences were and that they'd written their own material and wanted to get some gigs locally.

"They asked if I could get them a support slot at 'Improvision'. I told them that I didn't have any say in that department but I'd have a word with the Rank's general manager which is what I did.

"Nothing came of it. However, they did play the Rank at a later time as well as some of the biggest arenas in the world. The kid who did most of the talking was Joe Elliott.

"I squirm with embarrassment when I recall asking him what the band was called. Def Leppard, he replied. 'What a daft name', I thought, 'they'll never make it with a name like that'. Whoops !"

Pete Halliday, who ended up in Roadhouse with Pete Willis, said: "I used to be at school with Chris Clark, brother of Steve Clark. One day when I was about 14 years old Chris said 'do you want to see my brother's electric guitar?'. I said 'yes' and he took me into his bedroom and got it out from under Steve's bed and opened it up.

"He told me his band was called Def Leppard.

"We fell about laughing – 'Def fucking what?' we said? What the fuck's that all about.

"Steve Clark was also my prefect at school."

Chapter 5

From mining to MTV megastars - The Bailey Brothers

The Bailey Brothers in action in the early years

At least aspiring rock bands had some kind of formula to follow – even if the chances of global success were about ten million to one.

In terms of The Bailey Brothers' business model it was totally uncharted territory (and they'd be the first to admit they didn't have anything closely resembling a chart).

The 'superstar' DJ was well a over decade from being born and rock fans were, as far as Sheffield was concerned, working class and white.

The Bailey Brothers definitely ticked the 'working class' box (they were lining up for a life down the pit) but that was about it.

Their story is pretty incredible even for the fickle music industry and their rise to the upper echelons of rock saw them become a massive influence on the eighties rock scene both nationally and internationally.

Dez Bailey said: "When we came to Killamarsh [a suburb of Sheffield] we were the only black kids here.

Fortunately for us, all the older kids were into rock and the first albums we borrowed, off a guy called Mick Gregory, were Bachman Turner Overdrive's 'Not Fragile', Deep Purple's 'Deep Purple In Rock' and one from Sammy Hagar's first band, Montrose.

"The Sweet were also a big influence because their 'b' sides were really heavy.

"And that was it for our Mick. Every single penny was spent on it. But not only did he want all the English releases, he wanted Japanese versions, you name it!"

Mick Bailey said: "I used to get my records from Bradleys on Fargate and I knew someone there that would give me discount and I bought that many at that time I was spending my rent money and getting into debt because I was buying absolutely everything that came out."

That was in the mid-seventies. Their first DJ gig was May 13, 1977.

Dez said: "Mick was buying all these records and these imports and everyone was piling round to my mother's house to listen to them. It was our mother that bought us our first DJ set up.

"We hired Killamarsh Village Centre and sold it out – our first gig!"

At that point they weren't The Bailey Brothers, they were rather less succinct 'Mick & Dez Bailey's Heavy Metal Road Show'.

"Dez said: "We started doing all the youth clubs and pubs and would give out any bullshit to get a gig!

"We'd be stood on the top of tables rocking out with glasses going everywhere and landlords would be shouting 'turn it down, turn it down, we can't hear ourselves think'.

"And we'd use Ted Nugent's saying 'if it's too loud you're too old' and we'd be

Early days for 'Mick and Dez'

getting barred everywhere. It was just chaos... absolute chaos.

"And you've got to remember there wasn't so much of a rock scene at that time, many of the venues were hovels and you were regularly struggling for somewhere to play.

"It wasn't until we got our big break with Retford Porterhouse where we secured a residency that things really went up a gear. That really was the club that did it because everyone came through there. Everyone that played at London's Marquee played there. Leppard, Maiden, they all played there. We had to do every Friday and Saturday night. Saturday was rock night and Friday was punk night."

Their lack of in-depth punk knowledge/ championing of that particular scene didn't, it appears, cause them any grief in keeping the dance floor full on a Friday night...

Mick said: "We'd get all the punk kids and say 'hey, come up here and pick what you want' and they'd say 'really – pick what we want?' and we'd say 'yeah'.

"And they'd say 'right – we want Ramones and Ruts' and we'd keep the floor full all the time!

Dez said: "And then we'd say check this out and we'd play them Motorhead and got them into that and then they'd start turning up on a Saturday night as well and hang out with us. By the time we'd done we'd got 200 people regularly queuing at 8pm on a Saturday night because that was the time we'd be playing all Mick's American imports.

"And that was one of the reasons we really took off at that point as much of the audience were still into Hawkwind and all old hippy stuff. We were bringing all new stuff in like Kiss and Aerosmith and starting to educate them in that, and later, in the New Wave of British Heavy Metal and helping to break new bands.

"Geoff Barton from Sounds invited us to their tenth anniversary party in London.

"We did our apprenticeship under 'Mick & Dez' for the first three years and then started as The Bailey Brothers after Retford Porterhouse.

THE BAILEY BROTHERS COMMAND
THE ROCK FESTIVAL STAGE

"We landed our first London gig at the Electric Ballroom and the promoter saw our 'Mick & Dez Bailey Heavy Metal Road show' title and said 'I'm not putting all that on' and he said 'you're The Bailey Brothers' and just put that on.

Mick said: "My friend Brian Frost from Mansfield was a joiner and he made about 100 plywood guitars and painted them up. And we gave them to all the people that were coming in. And the whole venue was just rocking with these guitars! And nobody had seen anything like it.

Dez said: "And our Mick had one with all these LEDs that lit up. But that wasn't enough for us as we'd been watching KISS so we got this guy to make a guitar with pyro in it so when Mick went 'for those about to rock' this rocket flew out.

"Unfortunately one night he trod on the lead and it fired at him and it burned him.

Mick said: "I was in a right state!"

But the odd burn here and there only fired up the Bailey's quest for metal mayhem.

Mick said: "We ended up taking the show to all major cities and people would be queuing in their hundreds to see this gig we'd built up. For two Sheffield lads it was pretty good going.

Dez said: "What really made us was when we landed a residency in London and we'd hire a full PA and lighting rig as big as any bands. By this time we'd got this coffin thing built, pyros, dry ice and everything and we'd even come out to our own intro tape.

Mick said: "We always looked to find something different. Any DJ can play tunes but we want to find something different."

Dez said: "We got such a massive following at Retford Porterhouse we'd be on, whether the band knew it or not,

The Bailey Brothers with Bon Jovi

for the headlining act's encore. We'd do backing vocals and be up there with cardboard guitars.

"And because we'd have done a two hour gig before a band came on the atmosphere would already be electric before they even came on.

"Graham Oliver from Saxon went to promoters MCP and said 'you've got to get The Bailey Brothers to open for us – we don't want a support band when we do Leeds Queens Hall, we want the Bailey Brothers'.

"The gig was in front of 5,000! MCP said 'fucking hell, you're good at this' and we said 'give us a crowd and we'll give you a show'.

"And then it kicked off all round the country with them.

"Musicians like Lemmy would come down and see us and we'd all end up doing the Hokey Cokey!'

"Then we got this call from the bass player of Angelwitch, Kevin Riddles, who said 'you're on the front cover of Time Out! And we said 'what's Time Out?' and he said 'you don't know what fucking Time Out is – it's the biggest fucking magazine in London?!'

Fans of The Bailey Brothers make good use of the plywood guitar delivery

"It's headline was 'Why are these men playing cardboard guitars?'

It was the brothers' early success with Saxon that persuaded them it was time to give up mining for good.

Mick said: "I don't know of any other DJs that were doing anything like that in 1980. We came through on the New Wave Of British Heavy Metal but were established before that.

"We gave a lot of bands a break. Whilst we were playing Led Zeppelin we'd also be slipping in the likes of Diamond Head before they'd broke.

"We were the first people to play Bon Jovi over here – nobody had ever heard of them.

"We were also the first DJs to ever play in Rock City in Nottingham – we worked with The Sweet, Ian Gillan and loads of others that we'd looked up to.

"Bands used to come and stay here with us. I've had tour trucks stretching right down the street. Don Airey, Rainbow's keyboard player, he came here and we took him to the Admiral Fish Shop down the street in Killamarsh.

"The headline in Metal Hammer was 'best fish I've ever had'! If a band was struggling and couldn't afford hotel rooms we'd happily put them up.

"Nothing will ever touch the 1980s for music. Your Aerosmith, Def Leppard and everyone were hitting the big time and thirty years on they're still going strong.

Dez said: "I'd definitely put Leppard's Hysteria down as one of the best albums ever recorded. We saw Leppard at the very beginning – they played at our school, Westfield.

Mick: "I used to buy a lot of records from Revolution on Castle Market and Pete, the owner, was Leppard's first manager.

Dez: "We've played everywhere in Sheffield: Genevieve, Marples, Dingwalls, Penthouse, Limit, KGB on Abbeydale Road,

"It was the New Wave of British Heavy Metal that really turned rock music on its axis and brought your Iron Maidens through. Everything before started sounding old. There was the fresh energy of bands like Motorhead, Saxon, early Leppard and Diamond Head. It made the prog rockers really sound like dinosaurs and brought a lot of new kids in.

"We ended up with residencies in Birmingham, London, Wolverhampton,

Mick Bailey (centre with hat) with Def Leppard

Leeds – we were working six nights a week and hardly in Sheffield.

"We tried to do too much when we started working for MTV. We didn't want fans to think we'd left them out and continued doing our residencies and wrote for Metal Hammer. It was silly, it really was too much. There's enough work in organising a TV show every week.

Mick said: "This record company took us to Cologne in Germany to watch Tokyo Blade who we'd played with loads of times at Retford Porterhouse. Anyway we jumped up on stage with them for the encore and the promoter said 'you guys are fucking brilliant – do you want to play at my festival?'

"It was in front of 15,000 with Metallica, Wishbone Ash, Nazareth – it was a right set up. They booked us in a hotel and agreed to supply DJing equipment. We get there, all the bands are sound checking but there's no sign of our gear. And we shouted 'Manfred, we can't see any gear and we're on in an hour – what's happening?'. And he said 'no you were bringing the gear' and we said 'no, we're bringing the albums and you were bringing the gear'. He thought and said 'you're right – leave it with me'. Next thing, this contraption came up the drive looking like something out of 'Only Fools and Horses' on three wheels. There were two decks but only one worked together

With Status Quo

with a cassette player.

"There was a big piece in the programme about us and we spent at least an hour signing autographs before we finally went on. We were billed as 'Britain's wildest heavy metal DJs' and we just thought fuck it, we've got to go for it.

"We tried to do too much when we started working for MTV."
Dez Bailey

"We stuck Scorpions 'Rock You Like A Hurricane' on, got our guitars and launched ourselves over the barriers and into the crowd. That was 1985 – that was probably the first slam dive ever. It wasn't planned – we just did it.

"And they just loved us from that first track. There was a guy from Sky TV there and he said 'you know all the bands here – can you interview for us and they gave us the microphone' and we just did it on the spot. That was our first taste of TV.

"We sat down with the promoter after the show and he said 'that was brilliant' and he said they were looking to launch Metal Hammer in England. Back then

Bailey Brothers with Magnum and competition winners

there was only Sounds and Kerrang in the UK. Metal Hammer, in Germany, was as thick as a book.

"He said 'will you help us launch it and write for it?'

"We had full control of anything we wanted to do for years.

"When rock really kicked off MTV were looking for someone to front a show. They approached Metal Hammer about being sponsors. They asked Metal Hammer who should present it and they said 'there's only two guys that can front this – you need to get The Bailey Brothers in'.

"We had this big meeting with MTV and we had to do a screen test. We thought what the fuck we gonna do and then we thought, lets just go for it.

"The guy sat us down and said 'right who would you want to interview' and we said 'Dave Lee Roth. Well he said 'well I'm Dave Lee Roth, interview me'

"He came back after and said 'you guys are so natural on camera'. We ended up picking every single video and running the show as it was broadcast right through Europe. It had about 15 million viewers. We ended up being their number one rated show on hardly any budget. It was like Wayne's World!

"They ended up calling a specific board meeting one week to try and fathom out why we were so popular – the figures were going up and up and we were getting sacks of fan mail with 'rock not pop' written all over it. It was quite an achievement.

"The rock show started in 1988. We were on it nearly three years. It was

INTERVIEWING DAVID LEE ROTH

HEAVY METAL
HM charts
THE PORTLAND
BIRMINGHAM'S NEWEST LIVE VENUE
100 Icknield Port Road, Edgbaston.
MCP present
MON. APRIL 21st
BIG AUDIO DYNAMITE
plus support
£4.00 advance, £4.50 on door
Nice & Nasty Enterprises present
SUN. APRIL 27th
THE ROY WOOD BIG BAND
plus THE BAILEY BROS.
MCP present
TUES. APRIL 29th
THE BLOW MONKEYS
plus Guests
THE BAILEY BROS.
HEAVY METAL DEMONS
the marples
EVERY WEDNESDAY
Mr Lumpy's bone club
July 15th 'BAILEY BROTHERS' plus 'GRAFFITI'
July 22nd 'BAILEY BROTHERS' plus 'ALIBI'
July 29th 'BAILEY BROTHERS' plus 'ZAYUS'
Aug 5th 'BAILEY BROTHERS' plus 'JAGUAR'
DISCOUNT WITH DOLE CARD
MONSTERS OF ROCK
THE BAILEY BROTHERS
DONINGTON PARK SATURDAY 22nd AUGUST
ACCESS ALL AREAS
1987 MONSTERS OF ROCK
BON JOVI
DIO
METALLICA
ANTHRAX
W.A.S.P.
PORTERHOUSE
DEMON Plus The Bailey Bros
THE SWINGING LAURELS
TO BE ANNOUNCED
CHEETAH Plus The Bailey Bros
MAGNUM + The Bailey Brothers
ROMAN HOLLIDAY + Support
SOLSTICE + PENDRAGON
CHINATOWN + Bailey Bros
HANDSOME BEASTS
GRAND PRIX
"SPLODGENESSABOUNDS"
BAILEY'S ROADSHOW
"ANGELWITCH"
BAILEY'S ROADSHOW
"SAMSON"
REBELS
NO 1 ROCK CLUB
20–22 Dixon Lane, Sheffield
ROCK 9.00 p.m. to 2.00 a.m.
MONDAY 2nd & 4th Week of the Month
Alternative ROCK MUSIC
FREE ADMISSION
WEDNESDAY
ROCK – HARD ROCK – AOR MUSIC
50p Admission
£1 Drinks
THURSDAY
ROCK – HARD ROCK – AOR MUSIC
50p Admission
£1 Drinks
FRIDAY
ROCK – HARD ROCK – AOR MUSIC
£2.50 (before 11.30 p.m.)
£4.00 (after)
SATURDAY
AMERICAN ROCK
£2.50 (before 11.30 p.m.)
£4.00 (after)
REBELS ROCK DJ'S
LES (The Rebel)
VIKING MARK
DADDY
(From the Derby Rock House)
MARK DALE
ANDY COPPIN
THE BAILEY
The Bailey Brothers
DONINGTON PARK SATURDAY 20th AUGUST
ARTISTES
THE BAILEY BROTHERS
DEZ
NO1 POP

Europe's No. 1
MUSIC CHANNEL
IN ASSOCIATION WITH
BRITISH CABLE TV
FOR GREAT HOME ENTERTAINMENT
PRESENT
THE BAILEY BROTHERS & ROCK CITY
FRIDAY, 28th OCTOBER, 1988

FOR MORE INFORMATION ON MTV OR
OTHER CABLE TV CHANNELS
PHONE — ROCKLINE, NOTTINGHAM 622612
AND ASK FOR METAL MAUD
LUCKY PRIZE DRAW No. 00032

THE BAILEY BROTHERS LET LOOSE ON MTV

THE BAILEY BROTHERS IN NYC

BAILEY BROTHERS IN RECENT YEARS

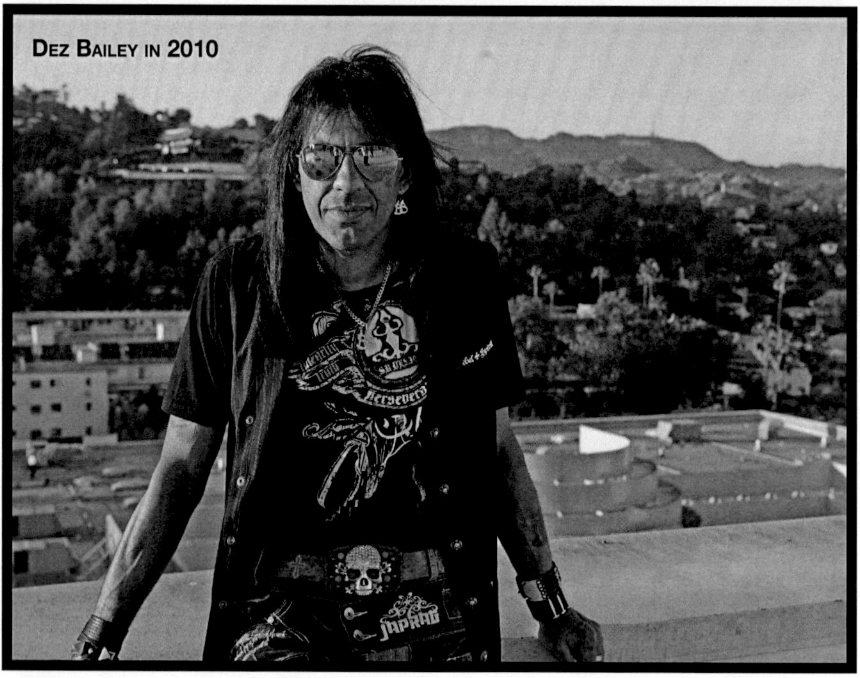

DEZ BAILEY IN 2010

With Motorhead

filmed in Camden and we did location stuff in France, Holland, Germany and then New York.

"What often gets lost in everything we've done is Mick's incredible knowledge of the music. "We'd mix every genre of rock so the dance floor never emptied and everyone went home happy. Music was always the main focal point, not us.

Mick said: "Walking on stage at Donington in front of 120,000 people was probably one of the highlights of my life. None of them gave us any abuse, threw anything at us and they all sang with us. The weight of everybody bouncing up and down and clapping was phenomenal.

Dez said: "When thrash metal kicked in there was a big divide at Donington. You'd got all your Cinderella-type fans and then your Metallica fans. Tony Wilson, who was a producer at The Friday Rock Show, turned to us and said 'I feel sorry for the first person on that stage'.

"We just walked on stage, grabbed hold of the mike and said 'what's all this shit – we're supposed to be one family – what's happening?' We managed to calm it all down and felt it was our role to do it. We felt they were all our mates because we'd done that many gigs around the country. We worked non-stop that day.

"And then in 1988, not only were we doing that – we were also interviewing bands as well. We had to interview every single band.

"One minute we'd be in a limo with Bon Jovi, next minute we'd be having a Tetleys back in Sheffield. We never really liked London that much but you had to be down there to make your name. It was shit beer and expensive.

"Rebels and Roxy were the Sheffield

CHRIS TWIBY SAID:
"A highlight of my rock years was meeting Mick and Dez Bailey in the Fleur de Lys pub in Totley one Friday. They were really nice blokes and true authorities on metal. Only 2 years earlier I had signed their petition at Donington for more 'Rock not pop' on Radio One. "They even made 100,00 people chant it."

RICHARD CHUMLEY SAID:
"I think people often forget the influence Sheffield's Bailey Brothers had on the metal scene of the 1980s. They were true one offs. If they hadn't introduced the UK to American acts like Bon Jovi the scene could have been very different."

venues that we hung out in the eighties. When you've got long hair you feel at home with people of your own type. Rock has always been like one big family.

"The manager of The Roxy told me 'we could open this with just two bouncers, we don't really need them as we never get trouble. I've not known a night like it'.

> **"Rock music totally died in the early 1990s. It was like a bulldozer went through it."**
> Mick Bailey

"I went to the court on crutches to try and get Capitol [the club that Rebels rock club ended up transferring its licence to] a licence. I got up and the judge said 'do you want to sit down' and I said 'not if I'm representing rock music, I'll stand up'.

"Leppard have got to be one of the highlights for me. No one but them would have stuck around for a one-armed drummer.

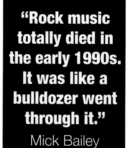

"When he lost his arm, Mick and me took a big card to Wapentake and got everyone to sign it for him.

"His first gig back in front of anybody was in the Nag's Head at Killamarsh

The Bailey Brothers felt the after effects of the rise of grunge as much as the next metal head...

Mick said: "Rock music totally died in the early 1990s. It was like a bulldozer went through it. Guitar solos and everything just vanished."

Bailey's Comet keep the bruvvers rocking into the 21st century

Things are still very much rocking in camp Bailey.

The bruvvers released an album as Bailey's Comet. Dez Bailey was song writer, guitarist and producer. They were described as a cross between Thin Lizzy and Whitesnake.

They're now working on a Bailey Brothers and friends album. Dan Reed has already asked to be a part.

Dez said: "For all our career we weren't the sheep. We were the ones that led the sheep. We were always one step in front.

"I like to think we've contributed immensely. When Leppard were nothing we were the ones playing them in London and putting their first EP in Sounds. Same with Saxon and scores of others."

Chapter 6

A Virgin on the Moor- Iron Maiden finds a true number for its beast

All-conquering Iron Maiden with Bruce Dickinson

Iron Maiden were originally formed 170 miles south of Sheffield in London.

By rights they should have failed. They formed in 1976 when punk was in the early stages of laying waste to the whole rock movement as grunge did to hair rock nearly three decades later.

They were named after a medieval torture instrument and the original line-up (bassist Steve Harris, guitarist Dave Murray, drummer Doug Sampson and singer Paul Di'anno) ended up centre stage, as a band fighting to keep the scene alive.

But far from indulging in the music excesses of the bands punk rock was killing off, Iron Maiden were far leaner and driven and had youthful energy that put them as flag bearers of the fast appearing New Wave of British Heavy Metal movement.

With no labels showing an interest they went the same way as Def Leppard and self-released, in their case it was the 'Soundhouse Tapes' EP which was championed by DJ Neal Kay.

They were signed to EMI after contributing a couple of tracks to the 'Metal For Muthas' compilation.

Their debut album shot to number 4 in the charts and was the first outing for their ghoulish, mad-eyed mascot, Eddie.

As the chart assault started so did the mission to take metal around the globe.

But their success with Di'anno, reckoned to be the most volatile of the group, was dwarfed with the arrival of his replacement, Bruce Dickinson, who was schooled in Sheffield.

His taste for rock, and his later career as an airline pilot, were initially fuelled by Sheffield's long gone Virgin shop that used to reside at the bottom of The Moor.

Dickinson's voice, quite rightly, was compared to the sound of an air-raid siren

He said of his early years in the city: "Saturday night out in Sheffield was northern soul night. There were clubs where you went and bought a pint and they gave you a knife with it.

"At the same time, there was the traditional blue collar where-men-are-men-and-sheep-are-frightened sort of things going on. Then there were the metal kids. We used to hang out in one of Richard Branson's first creations, the Virgin store. It was lots of joss sticks and patchouli oil and, funnily enough, aircraft seats to sit on. It may be how Richard came up with the airline idea."

Dickinson's voice, quite rightly, was compared to the sound of an air-raid siren and he held an impressive multi-octave range.

He cut his heavy metal teeth with various rock bands prior to Iron Maiden – the most notable being Samson that he joined in late 1979. He went under the moniker 'Bruce Bruce'.

With Dickinson at the helm, Iron Maiden now possessed stadium potential like never before.

Their 'Number Of The Beast' album put them in a different league. 'Run To The Hills' went top ten in the singles chart and the album hit the top spot.

It was the start of the band's golden period of the 1980s as hit record followed hit record followed by sell-out world tours.

Whilst the UK was in the midst of the Miners' Strike, Dickinson and his merry men were getting yet more ambitious – five sold-out shows at New York's legendary Radio City, performing in front of 200,000 in South America for the first time at the Rock In Rio gig and a visit to the Eastern Bloc.

Iron Maiden seemed virtually untouchable and notched up more hit albums and sell-out tours than most of us were having hot dinners.

Maybe it was the feverish pace of life in Iron Maiden that persuaded Bruce Dickinson to indulge himself in other careers that couldn't be further away from life on the road with the band.

He penned comic novel 'The Adventures Of Lord Iffy Boatrace' in the early 1990s; was invited to join the

MICK BAILEY (SECOND FROM RIGHT) WITH MEMBERS OF IRON MAIDEN AND DEF LEPPARD

DJ LEZ WRIGHT AT BRUCE DICKINSON'S 'SECRET' SOLO SHOW AT WAPENTAKE BAR. UNFORTUNATELY, BY ALL ACCOUNTS, IT WAS THAT 'SECRET' HARDLY ANYONE TURNED UP

Olympic fencing team (he was ranked seventh in the country as a swordsman at that point) and released solo album, 'Tattooed Millionaire'.

By 1993 the band were the wrong side of the tide that was turning against the whole rock movement.

Seattle and the rise of grunge seriously damaged the Iron Maiden machine and to make matters worse, Bruce Dickinson left to pursue a solo career.

Ex-Wolfsbane front man Blaze Bayley was left to pick up the poisoned chalice.

Despite a valiant attempt, Iron Maiden looked like being yesterday's news.

But the garden wasn't particularly rosy for Brucie either and in 1999 he announced his return – minus his flowing locks.

CHRIS TWIBY SAID:
"Reading Festival, 1980, was when Bruce Dickinson played with Samson (drummer in a mask in a cage...) and made Iron Maiden realise he was a much better singer than Paul Di'anno. The London bands (Maiden, Diamond Head, Angel Witch etc) were always seen to be favoured by the press and Dickinson joining Maiden was the final straw for some fans (a genuinely true story is a mate of mine who refused to go and see Maiden once Dickinson joined)."

MICK BAILEY WITH BRUCE DICKINSON

Wind the clock forward 10 years and Bruce Dickinson and Iron Maiden are bigger than ever and have successfully won over a new generation.

His hair isn't.

"I can now see where I'm going on windy days", he explained.

In the late 1990s they struggled to sell out Sheffield City Hall, these days they can sell out Sheffield Arena at the drop out a hat.

DJ LEZ WRIGHT SAID:
"Bruce Dickinson brought a solo album out and there was supposed to be a secret gig. Trouble is they kept it that secret there were only about 30 people. That was the Wap in Sheffield, just before it changed over to the Casbah."

REBELS FOLLOWERS IN ACTION

Chapter 7

Rebellion finds a home on Dixon Lane

DJ Ken Hall gets things rocking

Few rockers realised Peter Stringfellow had more than a little hand in the future launch of the region's undisputed king of rock clubs of the eighties and early nineties.

It was he that opened The Penthouse in 1969 in the space that ultimately became Rebels years later.

His love affair with the venue sited many floors above Dixon Lane didn't last long. If it had worked out for him there might have never been a rock club at all and Newcastle Brown would have probably gone out of business.

It was Peter Stringfellow's first foray into a venue with an alcohol licence and he should have cleaned up.

Unfortunately, or fortunately, if you were a burgeoning rocker, he cleared out, right out.

Beered up townies, it had to be said, weren't on Peter's list of wants at that point.

He'd already got an enviable rapport with major bands, having promoted everyone from The Beatles to Jimi Hendrix in the past. He'd built up a big following via earlier successes at his Mojo and Down Broadway venues in Sheffield.

Peter Stringfellow ended up selling the Penthouse business within months of opening.

It was, in his eyes, a disaster.

The club was at the top of flight after flight after flight of stairs – hence the name, The Penthouse.

The youngsters that had been his coffee-supping bread and butter at earlier ventures were now growing up and turning into a rather more potent mix – young adults with a thirst for alcohol which Peter was nicely lined up to sell.

And they were soon joined by a new crowd that headed to The Penthouse after a night's partying on Sheffield's rowdy West Street.

Peter Stringfellow said: "Down Broadway had been similar to the Mojo in that the crowd were young and didn't drink. I hoped they would follow me to the Penthouse, but instead I got an entirely different crowd.

PETE HALLIDAY (WITH BACK TO PICTURE) WITH A LOT OF HAIR

"Many of them had grown up in a Working Men's Club environment and were used to drinking, but they hadn't experienced drinking, dancing and live music. I began attracting the kind of clientele I should have never let in the place."

Like his previous two clubs, murals adorned the walls: Greek and Roman ones on the club itself whilst female dancing figures worked their way up the sides of the stairs.

Live music consisted of acts like Alan Bown Set who had been favourites at the Mojo.

Peter Stringfellow's mother regularly ran the box office with security provided by 'Big' Brian Turner and others.

Fighting became a consistent problem in the early days and Peter Stringfellow didn't hang around for long – he soon sold up, but The Penthouse carried on regardless under new ownership.

PENTHOUSE,
DIXON LANE
Every Monday and Wednesday,
FREE
with admission ticket to 10 p.m., 45p after.
It's Cheap Drink Nite
All drinks 18p
Don't forget, Get Drink at
THE PENTHOUSE

The venue ended up as a hard drinking rock club for most of the seventies – definitely not the vision of Peter Stringfellow.

Hen party nights, beat the clock nights – it was the second home for party animals everywhere but it was the rockers that made it their home more than most.

Ken Hall, best known for his years masterminding the decks at Wapentake Bar, started DJing there in 1975.

His playlist was a who's who of rock of the era. The likes of Black Sabbath, Deep Purple, Uriah Heep, Thin Lizzy and Status Quo kept the dance floor at fever pitch.

PHIL STANILAND SAID: "I was also a regular at The Penthouse in the late 1970s. Despite going in virtually every weekend in my early youth, the Xmas and New Years Eve nights seemed to be the most memorable for some reason.

"The Penthouse was the first place I saw rockers ecstatically flock onto the dance floor to songs such as 'Hocus Pocus' by Focus and 'Freebird' by Lynyrd Skynyrd and launch into a serious air guitar stance. More importantly - on further scrutiny some connoisseurs of the air guitar actually simulated the use of imaginary foot pedals before climbing up to the 12th fret for the solo and occasionally turning round and twiddling imaginary knobs on an imaginary amp head. Some of the chords they were doing were amazing – far more complicated than what was on the record!"

Rebels mainman Steve Baxendale who now runs Niche in Sheffield's Charter Square

DJ LEZ WRIGHT SAID:
"We had some great times. The coming and going of different age groups and different types of music was interesting. Different eras like glam rock and then your AOR stuff. Mid '80s was really good for the women. The dance floor was just packed out with them. When we came outside at the end of the night we'd regularly have people coming from other clubs to see all our women!"

MARK 'DJ MUTLEY' HOBSON SAID:
"STAIRS! Haircuts and rather dubious dress senses. Roz behind the bar. Meeting Ruth in the cloakroom. Sitting down with Chris Heaps and being told how silly I looked."

The Penthouse ended up falling out of favour and the venue reopened for a short time as Dollars.

The rockers ending up having brief spells at Stars on Queens Road and KGB on Abbeydale Road (under Abbeydale Picture House).

DJ Lez Wright, probably the best known of Rebels DJs over its lifetime, had The Penthouse to thank for his debut.

DJ Lez Wright said: "I used to go in the Buccaneer religiously and stand right in front of George Webster when he was DJing. One night I was standing there being mesmerised with singles going round and George went to the toilet. One of the records went off and it was sticking so I jumped over and did it for him. He came back and he says 'do you want to have a little bit here and there' so I said 'yes' and he showed me the ropes. An opening came at The Penthouse and I was recommended for that through George."

Rebels was the brainchild of ex-Limit bouncer Steve Baxendale. He was a biker and having his own rock club was a natural extension of things but he'd no idea how successful if was going to be.

Steve Baxendale said: "On opening night I thought no one had come. I came down the street and only saw four people outside. I was gutted.

"But then I opened bottom doors and over 1,000 people were on the stairs - all seven flights of 'em, brill.

"Major bands would come down from Sheffield City Hall like Def Leppard, Saxon and Meatloaf. It gave all the loyal fans a great memory mixing close up with their heroes."

The Rebels vibe was very much a good time all the time.

DJ Lez Wright is the first to admit the DJs did as much partying as the punters and the drinks flowed as much behind the decks as they did in front of them.

DJ LEZ AND COLLEAGUES

MANDI AND IAIN BARKER

He said: "There was one point in Rebels where they told me I couldn't have drinks behind the DJ box anymore. I got the face on and said I was leaving. I tried drinking orange for one night and I was diabolical.

"So the next night I went in and Steve said to me, 'Lez, have your beer behind here but don't let anybody else bring theirs - you're no good when you're not drunk'.

"Have your beer behind here...you're no good when you're not drunk."

"Well when you've had a few you get jumping about, get on the microphone and you can have a laugh. You've got to be on the same wavelength as your punters. But not too inebriated..."

Rebels had its fair share of VIPs over the years.

DJ Lez Wright: "I remember one night at Rebels little Mick behind the bar came up, he was bar manager and he says to me 'do you know who that is playing that space invader thing - Griff Rhys Jones!'

"I got a bit of paper signed to DJ Lez. He was doing something at one of the theatres and he came in because he likes rock music, apparently."

THE RETURN OF PETER STRINGFELLOW

Steve 'DJ Rude Dog' Rodgers said: "In the final weeks before Rebels closed I was working one Thursday and Peter Stringfellow turned up. The club had told him it was shutting and he wanted to see the club one last time. There was a fair few people in but not sure if they recognised him or not. I was there like 'wow this guy is awesome', so my manager waved me over and said 'go ask him if he wants anything playing'. So I went over and said 'hi, is there anything you would like playing?'

"He said 'no you're doing great. Love the fact you played 'Spirit in the sky', it's one of the first songs I played as a DJ'.

"So there he was dancing with a girl. At the end we chatted and he told us about how he used to have the place laid out when it was his club, the poker table here, another card table there, etc. I know in the press they take the mick out of him but he was so nice and genuine."

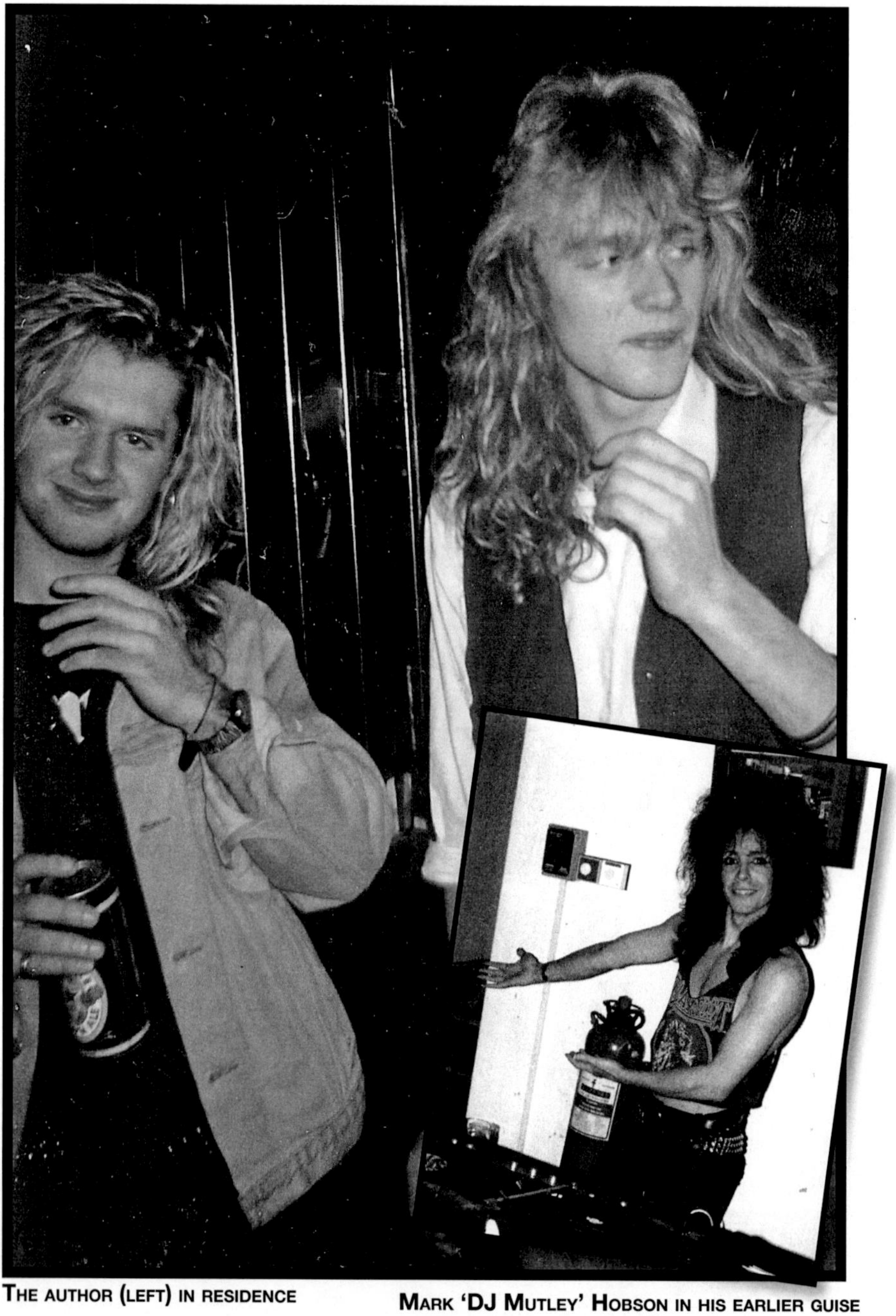

The author (left) in residence

Mark 'DJ Mutley' Hobson in his earlier guise as 'DJ Mark and his Kiss Katz Mobile Disco'

ICE-T AND BODYCOUNT'S VISIT TO REBELS

Johnny Loco, front man of former sonic city rockers Etiquette, said: "It definitely ranks as one of the most surreal evenings of my life... The day started calmly enough. We went up to the Kenwood Hotel in Nether Edge to interview Ice-T for a magazine.

"We had a good hour interviewing him and we got onto the subject of the whole touring band scenario where schedules don't give much time to seeing a town and all you normally see is hotel, tour bus, venue and that's about it.

"My band, Etiquette, offered to change all that and Ice-T was insistent we had to grab him at the end of their Octagon show.

"We caught their flash tour bus back to the hotel and they were nice enough to give us full run of their tab at the bar.

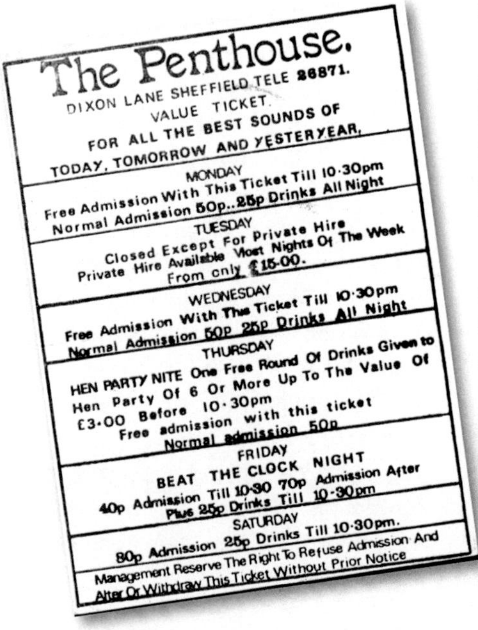
The Penthouse.
DIXON LANE SHEFFIELD TELE 26871.
VALUE TICKET.
FOR ALL THE BEST SOUNDS OF
TODAY, TOMORROW AND YESTERYEAR,
MONDAY
Free Admission With This Ticket Till 10·30pm
Normal Admission 50p..25p Drinks All Night
TUESDAY
Closed Except For Private Hire
Private Hire Available Most Nights Of The Week
From only £15·00.
WEDNESDAY
Free Admission With This Ticket Till 10·30pm
Normal Admission 50p 25p Drinks All Night
THURSDAY
HEN PARTY NITE One Free Round Of Drinks Given to Hen Party Of 6 Or More Up To The Value Of £3·00 Before 10·30pm
Free admission with this ticket
Normal admission 50p
FRIDAY
BEAT THE CLOCK NIGHT
40p Admission Till 10·30 70p Admission After
Plus 25p Drinks Till 10·30pm
SATURDAY
80p Admission 25p Drinks Till 10·30pm.
Management Reserve The Right To Refuse Admission And Alter Or Withdraw This Ticket Without Prior Notice

"Ernie C, their guitarist, and Ice-T, decided girls were high up on the agenda so Rebels seemed the obvious choice.

"I'm not quite sure what the club thought as 10 towering black Americans marched in with us. I think Lez the DJ got the picture. He started bellowing 'Bodycount are in the house!' Bodycount are in the mutha-fucking house!'.

"Despite Ernie C working the floor like a true pro the Sheffield rock girls didn't seem too enamoured by the thoughts of taking a member of Bodycount home so we agreed a Plan B was needed to woo our American brothers.

"Some bright spark mentioned Athena Sauna and the next minute there was a cavalcade of black cabs on route to Wolsey Road.

"I think the girls were a bit apprehensive. It wasn't their average Saturday night clientele. The funniest thing was various members of the band trying their hardest to teach us to say 'mutha fucker' in finest American twang.

"It wasn't so funny when the management got wind of it. We were all ordered out for swearing and Bodycount were definitely not in the house anymore that night.

"Within 24 hours we'd had calls from everyone from the News of The World to the NME. Everyone wanted to know about this bunch of upstarts from Sheffield that took Ice-T to sauna parlours and rock clubs. Quality!"

PHIL STANILAND SAID: "After ascending up the multi flighted and very steep staircase you entered the club on the top floor and paid through some kind of hole in the wall I seem to remember. Then you ventured into a dark black-walled one level room with music blasting out even beyond volume 11! It was a great club and not just popular with rockers. You'd always see a group of 'stray' townies or a bunch of hen party girls who at that stage in the night fancied something a little different to the 'norm'. In the DJ's box you had the 'unsurpassable Lez' at the controls giving the public exactly what they wanted. This being every rock classic under the sun delivered in a barrage of sound assaulting the senses along with Lez's memorable one liners over the mike such as "Come on Rebels Fuckin' Rock 'n' Roll!!!!!" And my particular favourite "Get ya coats from the cloakroom save the queue layyyyydaaaarrrrr!!!!!!" He always had a sidekick in the box with him who I think was nicknamed Woody.

"We had one very particular drunken night in there which got to be named 'Friday Bloody Friday'. Those present were myself, Andy C Beatson, Mark Johnson, Albert Theaker and Ike Glover. Both Ike and myself were in The Astrids at the time who were a kind of psychedelic rock band and were doing quite well on the local circuit. After visiting the usual haunts one Friday night i.e. The Foresters, Dickens, The Yorkshireman and Wapentake Bar we decided to end the night in Rebels. This is the night we discovered the Mad Dog 20/20 drinks. We had already had a skinful by the time we got to Rebels and the Mad Dogs just finished us off. We had spotted the 20/20s in the brightly lit drinks cabinet on the wall behind the bar. It must have been the garish colours that they came in that attracted us to them. There was plenty of madness and mayhem that followed several rounds of Mad Dog experimentation particularly on the dance floor.

"We always managed to be the last ones in amidst the broken bottles during 'sweeping up time'. I fell down on the edge of the dance floor damaging a few ribs but Albert took the crown for the rock 'n' roll casualty that night. While descending the infamous and formidable staircase Albert took a dive from about halfway down. He went flying past a few punters also on their way out and crashed from side to side against the walls like Morten Harket in the A-Ha video for 'Take on Me'. He then seemed to glide down in slow motion - head first and took a chunk out of the wall which left a dint near the club entrance with his head while breaking his wrist in the process. The 'dint' remained until the venue finally closed. Someone should have wrote on the wall at the side of it 'Friday Bloody Friday'. That wasn't all. Ike disappeared and Albert, Andy and Mark decided to get the same taxi and go to Mark's house at Hartley Brook Road. Albert's head was bleeding in the taxi and the taxi driver told him to cover it up with his leather jacket so it wouldn't stain the taxi seats!! When they got to Mark's, Andy slept downstairs where Mark's dog was and Mark slept on a bed which had a sunbed arched over it. This was the family home by the way. Next morning he appeared downstairs looking ill clutching a few of the damaged sunbed tubes in his hands but couldn't remember how that happened - and for some bizarre reason Mark's dog seem petrified and wouldn't go near Andy. What had he been up to during the night one may ask?

"Albert had to go to hospital shortly after. Furthermore when Andy came to use his car that day the petrol pipe had been severed rendering it useless so everyone came to some sticky end as a result of 'Friday Bloody Friday'. All apart from Ike it seemed who had simply 'disappeared'."

ENDURING METAL WARRIOR BEN DUKE (RIGHT)

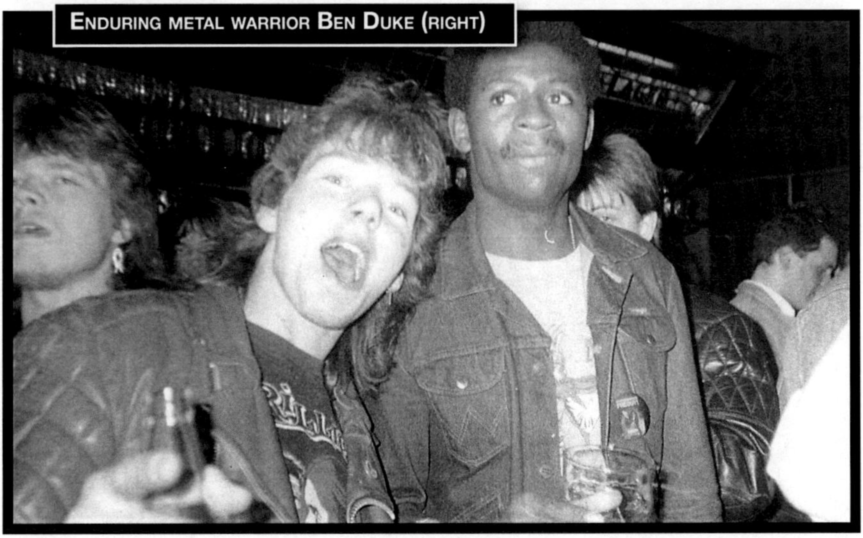

REBELS FOLLOWERS IN ACTION

KEVIN THOMPSON SAID: "First went when it was The Penthouse. Rebels, used to love a can of Special Brew with a Pernod dropped in, don't think I ever came out sober, normally Mon, Wed, Fri and Sat. Roxys, was that 1st Mon of month. What about KGB's on Abbeydale Road."

PHILLIP HACKNEY SAID: "Me and my bro' once made the drunken mistake of sitting directly next to the smoke machine... brilliant move for a mild asthmatic... :)"

STEVE POOLE SAID: "Thursday nights, wonderful times. A bus back to Chesterfield at 2.30am on Friday, home at 4(ish), up at 7 for work. Back for more on Friday and or Saturday."

JON HANSON SAID: "I fell down them stairs, pissed as a fart first time out in cowboy boots, and with a tin of Newcastle brown, never spilt a drop. fab times, long live Rebs."

Steve Cooper said: "USED TO LOVE THAT PLACE LOL...WISH WE COULD BACK IN TIME .....I THINK LOL...LONG LIVE ROCK 'N' ROLL."

NICK WALTON SAID: "Had my 18th there and got thrown out after drinking 4 cans of Special Brew with my friend Shaun before we went in,then making ourselves puke so we could drink loads of newcy brown when we got in. Was there one time and had no cash so got a job glass collecting but got the sack after half an hour for drinking other peoples drinks."

JAY GARRETT SAID: "Ah, trying to find my way back to Barnsley after 'New York New York........'"

PHIL ELWIS SAID: "After starting off in the Yorkshireman's Arms/ Wapentake Bar then drunkenly staggering down High Street I can remember drinking Newcastle Brown Ale beneath the UV lights of Rebels back in 1990, Jesus have you ever seen what Newcy Broon looks like under UV light, bloody scary!"f Head & Shoulders too!!I wish I could go back in time and Climb those Black stairs one more time, good times!"

MEL PEET said: "Remember when boyfriend at that time, Frodo, got on dance floor an asked me to marry him."

STEVE 'DJ RUDE DOG' RODGERS SAID: "It must have been '88/'89, because I used to swim for Sheffield. I always remember going out for my mates 18th birthday. Going up to the Frog and Parrot, having 'Roger and Out' and he puked his guts up and it was like, 'well, where are we going to go now?'

"And one of my mates had a brother who was into rock music and he said 'there's this club called Rebels, we'll go down there'. I just remember walking into this dark, dingy club and just looking at everyone, and going 'wow, these people look awesome - I want to look like this'.

"There were certain people I just remember seeing and thinking 'you look cool' and then I got to know them over the years. Such a weird transition. Nearly everyday I was training for swimming and then the next thing I was out on this night scene thinking 'there's a life away from swimming'. So it kind of dragged me into its dirty lair.

"It was kind of the end of swimming. I went to college to do art and graphic design and was kind of juggling my courses, my swimming, but then I wanted to go out at weekends. Sundays were training day and Saturday nights were partying nights. Going swimming with a hangover wasn't really working, so eventually I just had to quit swimming.

"Then I got introduced to the Roxy's Rock Night. The night we went, I would say there were a couple of hundred people there, not right busy. And then I didn't go for another year. When I was on the rock scene properly, when I used to go to Rebels, all my friends at swimming just carried on swimming and I didn't know anyone. So I used to go to Rebels on my own and just stand in this corner. Used to have these little round shades on the end of my nose and just watch everyone. I was a bit too shy to mingle. People used to see me, started to talk to me and I just got to know loads of people.

"I got to know a guy called Jerome, we were kind of talking and got to be good mates and then he said 'do you know that Lez has been sacked from Rebels?'.

And I was like 'no'. He said there were these guys called The Bailey Brothers who were going to take over. He said 'they want a DJ – do you want to give me a hand?'. And I went 'ok – I don't mind that!'

"So I remember turning up one night, and Rebels used to have a lot of its own records which we would use – all vinyl. We used to put the needle on the record and all that. We only did it for about three weeks, because the first week we did it we put all this good music on, and we got told off because it was like 'you're playing their set list'.

"So then they gave us a list of their set which we couldn't play. We started getting all these girls coming up saying would you put me this on, I'll give you a snog. And we were like 'alright then'. I just thought it was the best job in the world. You got to put great music on, you were getting snogged.

"We lasted a few weeks and what used to amaze me, the littlest Bailey Brother, he used to climb onto the DJ box and stand up on it. It was a ricketty old thing – you touched it and it wobbled. I kept thinking, it's going to break one day when you get up there mate.

"Don't know what happened with them, they were there for a while then left. Lez came back. And it was like that for a few years.

"Rebels was always the same, the same rock no matter what day you went on. Midweek it would be quiet. I talked to Sian, the manager at the time and just starting asking her if there were any DJ jobs going on. And she was 'there isn't now but I'll keep you in mind'. And on a Thursday there was a guy called Johnny and he used to love Faith No More, and because there weren't many people in the club - and I never saw this but I heard - the final straw was when he used to sit down, put a Faith No More album on, and just sit and read a newspaper. And that was it. So they asked me and my mate to come up with something. I think it was about the time when grunge took over/was taking over. People were wanting that old kind of glam rock and goth and punk stuff so we started to come up with something.

"It was like we're going to have glam, punk, goth and then we had to come up with a name. The manager said make your night an individual night so it's not just Rebels. We were trying to come up with a name and in one of The Damned's songs they mention 'Psychomania', so we came up with that name for the club night. They said to us 'go and get these posters done, if you design it, we'll print the posters'.

"We just started this Thursday night off, building it up and getting people in. I remember being late one night, and when we got there, they were like 'where have you been'. I was like 'sorry just been held up with traffic.' 'We've got a queue outside' and we were like 'yes, what's that about!!' So we now had a queue on a Thursday."

SARAH BARBER SAID: "EEEE them were the days! Half an hour to stagger up the stairs & 30 seconds to get down. I remember going after a knee opp & being held up by a bunch of rather nice youg fellas on the dance floor & getting Steve to play me some Ozzy :o)."

IAN WHINCUP SAID: "So many memories and a permanent scar. Four stitches in the back of me head. Thrown out after being asked to leave then falling completely arse over tit down the near vertical stairs. Happy happy days!!!"

NOELLA JEAN WOOD SAID: "I used to manage stairs by sliding down the wall but always ended up sitting on a greasy oil can at the side of kebab van at the top of the hill. Used to wake up with greasy oily rings on me dresses!!!"

LYNN NEVIN SAID: "Lots of hours of my life gone missing in Rebels after drinking Diamond White..happy days :)"

DEBORAH UNWIN SAID: "I used to go there all the time before 10 when it was free!! Had to go there because the Limit club closed!! I remember the stars and moons on the stairs and all the hairspray in the toilets. Best time of my life in that place! A shame it went, along with the Hornblower! Oh the tight leopard spot jeans (wouldn't get into them now). Rock On!!!"

ANDY ABBOTT SAID: "Miss my leather. dark blue Lewis leathers jacket, with Van Halen logo on the back in yellow and pale blue, think it was a guy called Jason that did it, a mate of Chris Percy. Got it nicked in Rebs one night when out with Steve Lister and "Billy" Wardle and Ron Walkerdine."

KAREN WALKER SAID: "Used to go in early '80s. Tried to go when it was the Penthouse but got kicked out for being under 18. Great place - met John Walker there and we've been married 23 years. Wish it was still open although I don't think I'd like climbing all those stairs!"

IAN HARPER SAID: "Some great times I had there 35p a bottle of Newcie Brown ,great music air guitars met loads of gorgeous women from '83 to '86 great memories and times!"

Rebels followers in action

Rebels followers in action.
Far right: Single release by Geddes Axe

PHILIP CUFFY CUTHBERTSON SAID: "I remember standing at the back, near Lez's DJ box, along with the rest of the thrashers, moaning about the music yet still getting up and headbanging to it! One of the worst days for Sheffield rock when that place closed. Many, many happy memories! Wish it would reopen, even if I would look really old there now!"

CHRIS TWIBY SAID: "Who could forget the family atmosphere, as if we were all one big rock community? A club that really stuck to its metal values. On a recent visit to Sheffield, we actually made a pilgrimage to the old site. My friend Jon was nearly in tears (but that could have been more to do with the Indian being shut)...

"I fell down the stairs a few times too. Joined in with the piano singalong in the pub at the bottom of the road and got my clothes from Pippys on Cambridge Street."

JOHN STABLER SAID: "Monday night free entry, Newckie Brown 40p a bottle until 10pm. So get bus from Chap at 9.15pm. Get into Rebels 9.45pm. Eight bottles of NB lined up round a pillar. Last all night.Then out to catch bus to Lane Top at 01.00 and walk back to Chap. Then they brought in the late buses on High Street which went at 02.15am. Glad it wasn't open on Tuesday, needed that night to recover."

KAREN MINORS SAID: "I was there from 1982 'til 1985 every nite it was open, then on & off till 1990-ish. Skin tight jeans, & blue leather jacket that was too big for me! Fantastic nights. Great memories. X"

LOUISE BULLARD said: "I remember Monday nights when it was cheap Newcastle Brown!! The hair and the spandex too!!"

SIAN THOMPSON SAID: "OMG Rebels days were some of the best of my life! I went from 1984 to around 1990 - happy days! The peeps I remember are Becca, Martin, Sandie, Tigi, Boop, Steve, Leo, Micci, Baby John, Chris Pye, Gary Whitehead, Pebbles, Keef, Chris Watson, Mutley and Ozz among others."

JOE BUTTERS SAID: "My week consisted of Monday night band practice, then the Wap and Rebels. Wednesday Rebels... with band practice (I think), Thursday band practice and Wap and Rebels, Friday was Wap and Rebels, Saturday was The Washington, then the Wap, then Rebels. How I did this on £40 a week I don't know... And I could still afford an LP."

ANNA HICK SAID: "'AHHHHHHHHHHHHHHHHHHHHH. Newkie brown. Really hard bouncers. Glammies getting hassle from thrashers for pullin' their girlies. Oh the joys of Rebs. Sticky seats and having your beer nicked. Smelly plastic trousers and Venom T-shirts (you know who you are) I miss the dump."

REBELS FOLLOWERS IN ACTION

Rebels regular Sally McLaughlan definitely lived life in the metal fast lane following a chance meeting with Guns N' Roses guitarist Slash at the band's Marquee gigs in London in the summer of 1987.

Sally McLaughlan said: "I didn't go to the show but went in for a drink. Not knowing who they were, I sat and shared a bottle of Jack Daniels with a 'nice boy' with curly hair.

"Anyone who shares their Jack Daniels is a nice boy in my book! After that a friend and myself went across the road to the St Moritz club where I saw him again. I remember getting hijacked into going to a party with him. We got into a car, Slash, me, Duff, Del James and Todd Crew (RIP)and headed off. They were an unsavoury looking bunch to say the least and I was a little worried about the outcome, so image how surprised I was when we pulled up outside the Ritz and headed into a party in Tom Zutant's (Geffen Records) Room. We were inseparable for the next two weeks, until he went home to LA."

Sally ended up moving to LA, partied with everyone from Motley Crue to Ratt and even starred in the video for Guns N' Roses' 'Sweet Child O' Mine'.

She's back in Sheffield these days but is still good friends with Slash and has nothing but fond memories of Rebels

Sally McLaughlan said: "I was 14 years old when we started going and used to go to school with hangovers! Coffee at first break!!! By the time I reached 18

STEVE 'DJ RUDE DOG' RODGERS AND WENDY DRURY

we were regulars and I was working for Steve Baxendale. "We danced most of the night, the DJs were fab and still are. "Steve used to pay me to enter the wet T-shirt competitions and get the other girls up to do it. That is why I always won! Plus I had great tits!"

SLASH (RIGHT) AND SALLY (SECOND FROM RIGHT)

SALLY AND SLASH IN MORE RECENT TIMES

Chapter 8

ALL GLAMMED UP AND SOMEWHERE TO GO - BARRY NOBLE'S OWN ALTAR OF METAL

Whilst Rebels happily catered for the rise of glam it always retained a grittier edge.

Its roots were in the first and second wave of rock and it never forgot it (or at least the battle-hardened punters that had been frequenting the venue since the 1970s wouldn't let them).

The Sheffield venue that truly took the hi-rise-hair by the horns was, bizarrely, Roxy: the sprawling mainstream club on Arundel Gate that was a byword for weekend carnage of the mainstream disco variety.

Seven bars, two dance floors and there weren't 79 flights of stairs to get in or out of the place (unlike its Dixon Lane metal counterpart).

The Roxy originally opened as the Top Rank Suite years earlier.Many Sheffielders still go misty-eyed as they remember acts such as The Ramones, The Police, The Clash, The Stranglers, The Jam, The Cure and Elvis Costello, who played there. Memorably, David Bowie brought Ziggy Stardust to the venue, one of three dates in Sheffield in 1972. Proximity to Pond Street bus station and the railway station meant it was a convenient location for customers from across the region. It could all sometimes get out of hand. Police recall the hazards of club-goers staggering late at night into the busy dual carriageway. Its Roxy incarnation attracted the likes of Kylie Minogue and Jason Donovan.

For a time, the name was 'Barry Noble's Roxy' in recognition of northern club owner Barry Noble, famed for his catchphrase "Is that alwright fer yusse?" His untimely death saw the title revert back to the Roxy.

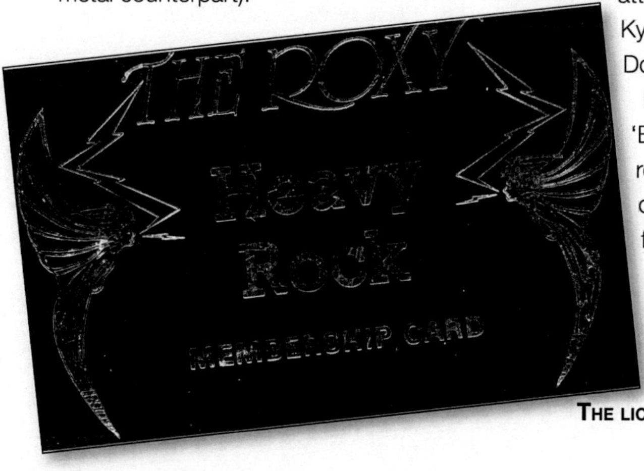

THE LICENCE TO ROCK!

Glam rock night at Roxy

It also hosted one of the worst TV programmes in the history of the entire world – Pete Waterman and Michaela Strachan's 'The Hitman And Her'.

Its only saving grace was the fact you were bound to be totally leathered when it appeared on screen around 1am on a Sunday morning.

Its Miss Glam Rock Competition became the stuff of legend

Roxy's Rock Night was a total phenomenon at its height and must have been a financial and trouble-free dream come true for the venue.

Its black and silver 'The Roxy Heavy Rock' membership cards were true badges of honour for the glam kids from across the region.

Sheffield could have definitely sustained a far bigger weekend rock club than Rebels, Roxy proved that, but the rockers were quite happy to have a change of scenery on Arundel Gate every other Monday and enjoy their more intimate home on a Friday and Saturday.

If they wanted bigger crowds on a weekend they'd be off to Rock City in Nottingham or the Mayfair in Newcastle.

The Roxy night, which started in 1987, was rammed to near capacity at its height – not bad considering it was held on a school night.

The night became one of the most popular bouncer shifts because the women were generally stunning and the only hint of trouble was the odd hissy fit in the gents.

We shudder to think how many work days were lost as a result of the countdown to the event (we know many a glam who would need an entire afternoon to get ready) and the hangover aftermath: it was definitely a plus to be the holder of either an NUS card or a UB40 in days of Roxy's Rock Night.

People would regularly travel from right across the country to the event and its Miss Glam Rock Competition became the stuff of legend.

Nearby pubs like the Mulberry Tavern and The Yorkshireman were packed to capacity and the trouble-free night was a far cry from the warzone that was the venue's normal weekend offering.

Graham Wild of Roxy said: "It was the Roxy management at the time that decided on a rock night. It was a couple of students that worked there at the time and were into rock themselves that suggested it and it took off from there. The management at the time were (general manager) Mike Powell.... and his (deputy manager) Kevan Dobson....They saw what was happening at the top of Dixon Lane and seized the opportunity to capitalize on the rock scene, this in turn increased the Monday night and in turn Wednesday night's popularity and vastly increased the people that turned up to Roxy's."

Miss Glam Rock winner Ruth Bowyer

The legendary Miss Glam Rock competition and contestants

DJ COLIN SLADE AND MISS GLAM ROCK WINNER RUTH BOWYER

PHIL STANILAND SAID:
"If I remember rightly there seemed to be a bit of a rock revival in the mid to late '80s which coincided with the Monday 'Rock Nights' at Roxy's (now the O2 Academy). These occurred on the first and third Monday of every month. This was a really great night but you had to be prepared for feeling rough for the following couple of days at work!!! It was a real curl up and die syndrome!! Radio Hallam's Colin Slade did most of the DJ-ing

"I seem to remember that he had probably left the radio station at this point. It was a very 'glammy' night that was attended by some of the most glamorous women who weren't necessarily 'real rockers' because you wouldn't necessarily see them in other rock pubs on other nights such as the Yorkshireman or the Sportsman.

"They must have just enjoyed the general 'vibe' of the event and probably liked the 'dressing up' aspect of it too. You could always differentiate between the British Telecom girls, the Dore and Totley residents and the real die hard full time rock girls you saw in Rebels.

"My particular soundtrack to these nights if I was trying to recall the songs played would be (and this is just a few off the top of my head) 'Sweet Child o' Mine' and 'Welcome to the Jungle' by Guns'n' Roses, 'Get the Funk Out' by Extreme, 'Yankee Rose' by David Lee Roth, 'You Shook me all Night Long' by AC DC, 'Gimme all Your Loving' by ZZ Top and 'Killing in the Name of' by Rage Against the Machine.

"I think there was a real 'golden period' between the late '80s and mid '90s when the rockers had never had it so good what with

JILLY BARKER SAID: "So much hair!"

ANDY NEILSON SAID: "We regularly came up from London in a van. Roxy's Rock Night was known right across the country's rock scene. The women were absolutely stunning. It was the best rock night in the country bar none."

CHRIS TWIBY SAID: "Roxy Rock nights...Double checking to make sure it wasn't gay night, sneaking whisky and vodka in my jacket pocket, tipping it into an empty can."

JACK TORRES SAID: "Roxy Rock Night was the ultimate glam night. We'd spend at least three hours getting ready listening to Motley Crue."

JAMES GLOVER SAID: "Monday night Roxy was mental – the women were out of this world and the blokes all spoke with American accents and wanted to be David Lee Roth or Jon Bon Jovi."

the available venues which also coincided with the general rock revival that existed for a while then. There was the Sportsman pub on Cambridge Street that had always been a home to the rock fraternity and which was known for its lunchtime rock discos played at excruciating but essential volume!!! There was Rebels nightclub, The 'Rock Night' at Roxy's, the classic Yorkshireman and the slowly fading but forever omnipresent stalwart of them all the Wapentake. The numbers were dying at the Wapentake but it still managed to maintain its foothold within the rock community.

"More importantly Olga Marshall was still the manageress which displayed a remarkable 'innings' on her part. There was also the short lived but good while it lasted 'Capitol' which was the result of Rebel's closure, and at some point Cuba that hosted a good Saturday rock night.

"Due to its small capacity Cuba subsequently moved its 'rock' operations to 'Kiki's', then to the Nelson Mandela student bar, and finally crash landed in Bank Street at what used to be the old Romeo and Juliet's under the name of 'The Corporation'.

"In subsequent years this would move to Milton Street where it still resides today."

Roxy's is actually inadvertently responsible for much of Sheffield's rock scene today via a 'DJ Mark' who auditioned for a spot at their rock night in the late 1980s.

Things could have all turned out very different for Mark 'DJ Mutley' Hobson, the man at the very helm of the scene today via his Corporation venue that sits proudly on Milton Street, if it hadn't been for a fortuitous phone call and a radical change of DJ moniker.

Mark 'DJ Mutley, Hobson said: "Roxy resident DJ Colin Slade was very much a radio DJ [he was on local station Radio Hallam] and they wanted to glam up the music. I applied and got the job but I nearly didn't.

"I was 'DJ Mark' at the time and it turned out there were at least two other people going under the 'DJ Mark' moniker at the time.

"I never heard back after the audition so, eventually, I decided to haul myself over to the phone box and ring them."

He was greeted with a pretty matter of fact answer.

"They told me 'we've already told you – you start in two weeks time.'

"It turned out another 'DJ Mark' had rung them on the off chance of getting some work, they thought it was me and he was lining up to play."

'DJ Mark' two must have thought all his heavy metal birthdays had come at once before the mistake was rectified.

Mark's 'DJ Mutley' was quickly born out of necessity and the future rock powerhouse had arrived.

He said: "I quickly went on to play in Nottingham, Wolverhampton, London, Sunderland – all over the place."

Grunge signalled the end for the Roxy Rock Night in the mid-1990s but it didn't go quietly.

It tried live acts and all kinds but the writing was on the wall for Sheffield's glam days of the 1980s and 1990s.

Metal madness

CAROLINE GOWING SAID:
"Sheffield provided a big night out for us Chesterfield metalers, Rebels and Roxy's were a treat if we had enough cash to visit the big smoke. Actually we never did have enough cash but we'd go anyway, take our own drinks in or hope someone would buy us a drink. The Roxy's rock nights were crazy, crazy, crazy, crazy nights! The Sheffield rockers seemed to have bigger hair, wilder clothes, and the glammies wore more make-up. I remember the night 'The Power Hour' TV programme was being filmed from the Roxy's, it was really exciting to be part of it and there were loads of people in that night, many more than usual. At some point during the evening, I met Krusher the presenter and he invited me up to his private roped-off bar area upstairs. He said I could order whatever I wanted from the free bar, and come and join him at his table. I was a bit scared to be honest, I was only a teenager and he was much older than me. So, I asked for a tray at the bar, ordered as many drinks as I could carry and legged it back to my mates! I spent the rest of the night avoiding him – sorry Krusher!"

ROCK SOUNDS FROM HOWARD SRTEET

Sheffield even boasted its own dedicated rock music shop when the scene was at its height. Powerhouse on Howard Street built a loyal clientele and attracted major names through its doors like Tigertailz and Celtic Frost for signing sessions.

TIGERTAILZ SIGNING ALBUMS AND MEETING CAROLINE GOWING (TOP RIGHT)

CELTIC FROST IN POWERHOUSE RECORDS

ROXY ROCK NIGHT IN FULL SWING

MAKE-UP REGULARLY BECAME FAR MORE POPULAR WITH THE GENTS THAN IT DID WITH THE LADIES (BOTTOM SHOT)

Chapter 9

SEMINAL GIGS AND METAL MARAUDERS FROM AROUND THE REGIONS

ROBERT PLANT ON STAGE AT WEST STREET'S LEGENDARY LIMIT VENUE

No metal tour of the 1980s was complete without a gig at Sheffield City Hall. It was an absolute bastion of metal. Over 2,000 rockers going hell for leather on three levels (not forgetting the sprawling bar underneath).

The place stank of patchouli oil (the perfume of choice for any rocker worth his salt in the late seventies – male or female) for days after and no Wrangler denim jacket was complete without 50 or so patches depicting your fave bands (you could get away with less if you had a big one that covered the entire back section).

Afghans were allowed but they were a bit of a hippy, sixties throw back – being a Led Zeppelin fan would probably point you in that direction.

Lewis leathers were the motorbike jacket of choice and Pippy's (which used to reside on Cambridge Street within spitting distance of the Wapentake Bar) was the place to purchase everything clothing and aroma-wise.

Sheffield City Hall didn't have the easiest of initiations – it was definitely not built for knobs being cranked up to 11 when it was unveiled in 1932.

It jockeyed for prime position with Top Rank and both universities but packing out Sheffield City Hall was always the ultimate goal to impress the parents if you were born and bred locally.

Led Zeppelin, Deep Purple, Black Sabbath and the majority of flag bearers from the first wave of rock in the seventies all played landmark shows.

By the eighties it was the time for the NWOBHM to flex its muscles in the hallowed hall of rock and then, as a result, it opened the floodgates for thrash, AOR, hair rock and other guitar heroics of metallic persuasion.

If they weren't ready for Sheffield City Hall, it was Snig Hill's Black Swan catching many of the early bands on the up in the seventies.

MICK RONSON AT SHEFFIELD CITY HALL

Reg Cliff caught AC/DC in the heady days before the arrival of Brian Johnson.

He said: "Bon Scott was the lead singer and he had the audience mesmerised. When they came on it was still light and you could see through the windows out onto Snig Hill. A bus pulled up outside, I think it was a number 88! AC/DC finished a song and as the applause died down, Bon Scott spotted the people on the top deck of the bus peering in and he screamed out, 'hello everyone on the bus'. Hilarious to see the astonished faces of the bus passengers as they wondered what this bare-chested rock singer with long hair was doing."

Few could beat Bruce Dickinson and Iron Maiden for pure size of show according to the venue's legendary former head of security and total metal obsessive, Robbie Bifield.

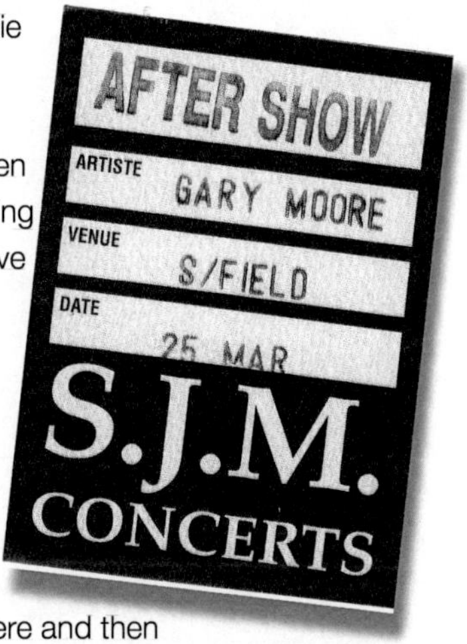

He said: "Iron Maiden used to bring between five and seven artics plus their own generator. They were the biggest that we had there and then they started with Mr Eddy. One bloke in that. It came in two parts. They did a two nighter one year and we helped them clean it up - it was fucking big and heavy.

"But an excellently brilliant show Maiden."

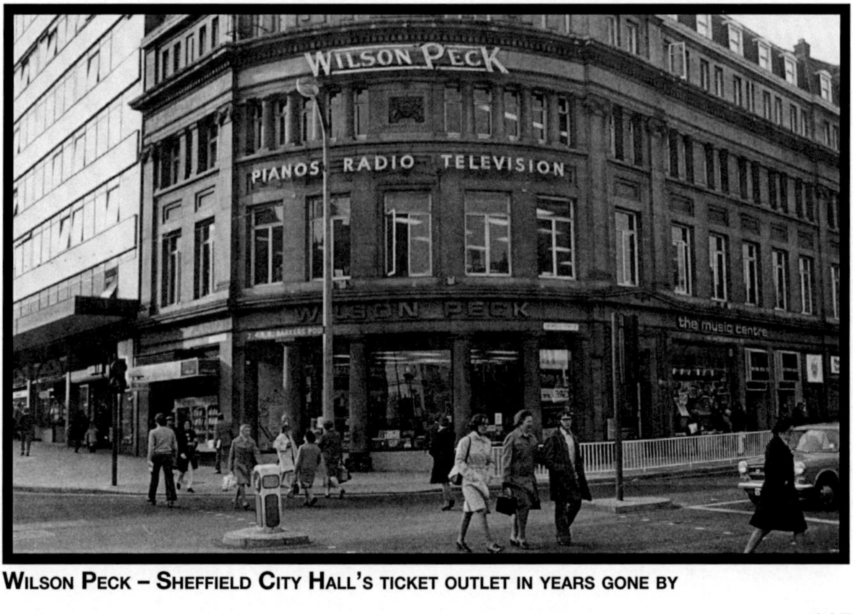

Wilson Peck – Sheffield City Hall's ticket outlet in years gone by

BLACK CROWES LEAVING SHEFFIELD CITY HALL'S STAGE DOOR UNDER THE WATCHFUL EYE OF HEAD OF SECURITY ROBBIE BIFIELD

Sheffield has also had its fair share of the wild and wonderful including everything from Jane's Addiction at Take Two (a tiny venue that used to exist in the city's Attercliffe area – a suburb hardly noted for legendary rock'n'roll gigs) to Robert Plant at The Limit.

Robbie Bifield said: "Judas Priest was one of the first bands in the country to do two lead guitars with Ken 'KK' Downing and Glenn Tipton. They were really out of this world. Another guy I liked was Alice Cooper. He used to tell a story all the way through and the first time we had him, near the end when he got hanged, they had dwarves take him off. He then came back out in a white suit and played 'Schools Out' and they had these big balloons with false blood in them.

JOHN ALFLAT WITH WHITESNAKE'S DAVID COVERDALE

"Well you push them out, they pop and there's blood all over the place. Everyone's coming out covered in blood and they absolutely loved it. It stained the seats. How they got the fucking stuff off I don't know."

Man-mountains Manowar and their 'death to false metal' crusade came unstuck in Steel City.

Robbie Bifield said: "One of the worst bands I saw were American – Manowar. Fucking posers they were fucking wank. I mean the way they posed on stage, like two guitarists would lean back to back to each other. I thought for fuck's sake give up."

Meatloaf fared rather better.

Robbie Bifield said: "Another nice guy, not metal but rock, was Meatloaf. He never used to know when to come off stage. He would do a three hour gig. And one night, he was on stage, it wasn't the 'Bat Out Of Hell' tour, it was his next tour. We didn't even open the doors until 9 pm – they should have been done at 7pm. But he was such a fucking perfectionist to get the sound right he would not do it until it was completely right.

"But what a stage show he used to do. It was really good. I spoke to him quite a bit."

It was a dream job for a lover of metal like Robbie Bifield.

He said: "I was lucky. I was in the right position at the right time.

"Another band that interested me was Europe. They had a couple of hits, 'Final Countdown' and 'Rock Tonight', but their gig was disappointing. But that was only me. Other people said it was brilliant. Maybe I got to be too complacent, I wanted perfection.

"Another guitarist, Gary Moore, brilliant. Not a big light show, but the sound and the twist of his face when he plays that guitar. You will never see a guy pull so many faces when he is playing a guitar, but brilliant music and the sound was good.

"You got to see the same faces at all the heavy metal gigs. And they would not only come from Sheffield, they would come from Nottingham, Derby. A lot of fans used to follow the gig round. I can't even count on one hand the trouble we had with heavy metal. I don't think we ever did since we took over the security at the front of the stage.

"They just enjoyed the music. Head banged. Didn't cause trouble. Never wrecked the place."

MR BIG'S PAUL GILBERT SIGNS AUTOGRAPHS AFTER THEIR SHEFFIELD CITY HALL SHOW

MR BIG'S BILLY SHEEHAN BACKSTAGE AT SHEFFIELD CITY HALL

CLUBBED TO DEATH

Rock nights were rife across the region as glam metal hit the charts in the mid 1980s. Every pub worth its salt decided it was time to cash in.

But for all their efforts, Sheffield always retained its crown as the epi-centre of the scene.

Caroline Gowing talks about rock life in nearby Chesterfield – things of a similar nature were being played out in Rotherham, Doncaster, Barnsley and other nearby towns at that point.
She said: "Going out on the rock scene in Chesterfield when I'd just left school was a massive influence on me at such an impressionable age. I wouldn't be the same person without meeting those people and sharing those experiences. The way the rock environment brought together its own community in town was unforgettable. If you wanted to get together with like-minded people all sharing a common bond through their love of loud heavy metal music the Anchor pub on Lordsmill Street was the place to go. There were all different varieties of rock fans like thrashers, greasers, glammies, bikers, goths, all ages from underage teenagers upwards. It was great fun, folks all got on well and there was rarely any trouble like there was in some of the trendy bars and discos. The Anchor was packed at the weekends, but any night of the week there was always a friendly face in there. Harvey Hill, the landlord made everyone welcome with his cheerful service and provided the music we all wanted to hear. Many of the local rockers had their own bands which were hosted at the Anchor and at the Greyhound over the road and at the Adam & Eve rock nights. It was a very special time. There were some real characters around, particularly the boys in bands who dreamed of living the rock 'n' roll lifestyle and developed unique identities.

"The Adam & Eve nightclub was aptly named for me because it was where

GERRY LAFFY, Girl guitarist alongside future Def Leppard man Phil Collen, has interesting post gig memories outside the back of Sheffield City Hall: "As we came off stage after opening for (and going down well with the Sheffield headbangers) UFO there was an altercation. Some Sheffield lads decided they needed to teach the lipsticked fag boys from London a lesson. Sadly for them they threw the first punch at Phil Collen, bing bang boom, as me, Phil Lewis, Simon (my brother) all steamed in.

"The hard nuts from Sheffield must have felt the same as the Cardiff lads who notoriously last year got hammered on cctv by two cage fighters dressed in drag for a stag party... happy days."

it all started. The rock nights, music, people and atmosphere were a great introduction to the rock world for a teenage rebel. The place was bursting with long haired rockers, full of smoke and mirrors and dark seedy corners. It had a tiny dance floor packed with headbangers, people playing air guitars, sliding on their knees or moshing to something thrashy. It didn't matter how hot and sweaty it got, nobody took off their leather biker jackets because they were essential to look cool and it was so dark in there you would probably never find them again. You never used the cloakroom, because you had to pay, money was so tight and every penny was needed for the bar. The beer was cheap but tasted watered down so pints of lager/cider snakebite were the order of the day, to disguise the taste or work its magic quicker. Most of us smuggled in our own drinks like bottles of Thunderbird shoved down the linings of our biker jackets - the bouncers were quite easy to get past on the way in. It didn't matter how dodgy the place was, its character was such that you could go wild and have as much fun as you could handle carefree."

SKID ROW - SHEFFIELD CITY HALL

CAROLINE GOWING SAID:
"It was Skid Row's first headlining tour of the UK, their self-titled debut album had just come out earlier that year. There was a lot of excitement when it was announced glam rockers Vain were the support act as their album 'No Respect' had also just been released and both bands were had popular hits at rock nights. Skid Row's anthem 'Youth Gone Wild' was a particular favourite, a track about rebellion and living the rock 'n' roll lifestyle. Great sentiment, which seemed appropriate at the time but ironic now, as I'm picking up my long service award for 20 years in the company next week! I was lucky enough to get tickets for the downstairs circle and with no regard to the allocated seat numbers, everyone piled down the front in a wild heaving, jumping heavy metal crush. The tracks from the Skid Row bootleg gives you a feel for the disorderly teenage enthusiasm, fuelled by Sebastian Bach's outrageous expletive banter and rock n roll attitude, encouraging infectious crowd chanting with plenty of 'F' words! It's quite funny hearing him slagging off the mainstream bands of the time like Bros and Milli Vanilli! It was great to see Skid Row at the City Hall before they went on to tour the arenas with Motley Crue."

BEN DUKE, ONE OF THE MOST PROLIFIC ROCK GIG AND CLUBGOERS SHEFFIELD HAS EVER KNOWN, SAID:
"I remember the '80s rock scene in Sheffield very well. There was a covers band called Spoilt Rotten who had a guitarist called Sean Creasey who I now understand is a very well regarded sessionist, who does film scores and adverts and theme music for TV, something like that, he has his own studio in London, done very well for himself. I understand that Mel Gabbitus was in a covers band and also has a studio in London. Mel Gabbitas has also done some session work for I think Ian Hunter's daughter amongst others.

"There was a covers band called Bastion who were a very good Metallica covers band. I remember them and Spoilt Rotten playing the George IV on Infirmary Road in Sheffield. I remember slam diving at Exodus, Nuclear Assault, Kreator, Napalm Death gigs mainly at the Lower Refectory, University of Sheffield campus in the '80s! Local band Amnesia also played the Lower Refectory after they got a record deal on a small independent label.

"I remember going to see Thunder supported by Electric Boys at the Lower Refectory complete with the power cut of the day. They were good nights. I remember going to see Strongheart at the Penguin in Shiregreen in the '80s. "That were a couple of good gigs. I remember going to see Def Leppard, Haze, Black Mariah and a few other bands at the Wapentake pub (The Wap) in Sheffield, now called The Casbah. Haze were a very good progressive rock local covers band.

"They played most of Sheffield's pubs that put rock bands on including the Hallamshire on West Street. I had many a good night watching Haze who were an excellent band.

"I also saw a local band called the Plague Dogs and an early version of Apes, Pigs and Spacemen play the Hallamshire. These were good nights at The Hallamshire, where lots of local bands played and you could see how various players were progressing.

REG CLIFF, DJ AT TOP RANK (WHICH LATER BECAME ROXY), SAID: "'Improvision' was the name given to gig-based Sunday nights at the Rank from about 1977 onwards. There had been Sunday night gigs before that, but I think that the management invented the name 'Improvision' to give Sunday night a stronger identity. I deejayed most of the Sundays and the bands were principally new wave or punk with some heavy rock too. AC/DC, Judas Priest and Styx all played there."

Why did the fans queue all night?

THE queue — and the end is "out of sight"! Just part of today's crush for tickets.

ANSWER: THEY WANT TO SEE LED ZEPPELIN

LED ZEPPELIN MANIA hit Sheffield today! And the fans were showing their devotion to the pop group two months before they are even due to arrive in the city.

To make sure of a ticket for Zeppelin's City Hall concert on January 2 some fans queued all night in the cold and rain outside Wilson Peck's in Leopold Street.

By the time the doors opened at 9 a.m. this morning the queue had stretched right round into Barkers Pool and alongside the Grand Hotel building.

First fan on the scene was Robert Ramania, aged 16, from Montague Street, Doncaster, who arrived at 10.45 last night.

"I wanted to make sure that I got a really good seat and the only way to do that is to get here early," he said.

He arrived with his friend, Robert Cottrell, also 16, and from Wheatley Hills, Doncaster. The lads braved the elements on one of the worst nights since last winter with a plastic bag to help keep them dry!

For their efforts they were rewarded with a free copy of the group's latest album by Wilson Peck's.

"Anyone who stayed out that long, especially last night, deserves it," said the assistant general manager, Mr. J. F. Rowan.

What is so special about Led Zeppelin?

"They are the best rock band in the world," said Colin Coomer, aged 17, who has been an ardent fan of the group for some time. He and his three friends arrived early this morning from Pontefract armed with folding chairs, flasks, sandwiches and warm clothing.

Further along the queue was a devoted mum chasing a ticket for her schoolboy son. "He couldn't come because he had to go to school, so I'm standing in for him. My friends wi' think I'm mad," she said.

Tickets, priced at £1, were being limited to two a person to stop black market dealings.

"The Yorkshiremans (Arms) was a great second drinking place after starting off at the Wap! Especially on the 1st Monday of the month which is when everybody that was into rock music made their monthly pilgrimage to Roxy's.

Everybody dressed up special for this event. Roxy's drew people in from as far afield as Hull, Grimsby and Scunthorpe. Roxy's played all the glam of the day such as Dog's D'Amour, Love/Hate, LA Guns and thrash metal bands that were coming through such as Slayer, Anthrax and the more established Metallica.

"People's outfits were fantastic, especially in those big hair glam days! Sheffield's main rock club was The Penthouse which was subsequently renamed Rebels. Rebels was situated above a department store near Sheffield Castle market. I've had many an excellent night in Rebels and all Sheffield's rock fraternity regularly visited Rebels. Leadmill nightclub had a few rock bands on over the years slightly more in the '80s than they do now. I saw Live play their first UK show at the Leadmill and this was broadcast over to the USA. I saw Love/Hate play an excellent gig at the Leadmill in the '80s. Many up and coming bands that would go on to be stadium filling bands played the Leadmill, cutting their teeth, playing mid afternoon as part of a six or eight band bill! These bands include Body Count, Faith No More and the

THE LATE PEPSI TATE OF TIGERTAILZ ON STAGE IN SHEFFIELD

Red Hot Chili Peppers to name but a few. Sheffield Polytechnic Campus now called Sheffield Hallam University used to put bands on in a venue called the NMB (Nelson Mandela Building). In the '80s I saw Faith No More, Gun, T'Pau at the NMB amongst others. "I saw Judas Priest supported by Iron Maiden at Sheffield City Hall in the '80s. Sheffield City Hall was Sheffield premier venue for big rock bands in the '80s, way before Sheffield Arena was built. I saw practically every rock and metal band at Sheffield City Hall in the 1980s. I've had so many good nights at Sheffield City Hall it's untrue. Genesis with an early version of 'In The Cage' drum solo medley, sticks in my mind coz I didn't even like Genesis 'til I went along! AC/DC Back in Black tour, first tour with Brian Johnson! Motorhead supported by Saxon! The roof came off when Metallica played on the Puppets tour 1986 supported by Anthrax! Still one of the best gigs I've ever seen! I remember that night clear as day, coz I found a tenner on the Rebels stairs after the gig! A lot of money in 1986! Take Two was a venue up Attercliffe just off Staniforth Road. I thinks it's biggest claim to fame was Jane's Addiction played in '87 or '88!"

NIGEL LOCKWOOD SAID:
"New Year's Day, 1978, the Heavy Metal Kids [rock/punk crossover act fronted by future Auf Wiedersehen Pet star Gary Holton on vocals] played Top Rank in Sheffield.

"They all turned up at my house in Woodseats wanting to crash. It was 3.30am and they were all parked outside.

"I'd got my mum and dad asleep in the house."

Chapter 10

OTHER ROCK HITS, MISSES AND METAL NOTABLES

Though the percentage chance of another regional rock success the size of Def Leppard coming along in the eighties (or any other decade far as that goes) was about two million to one, it didn't stop hundreds of other acts giving it their best shot.

When you compare the career prospects for the majority of the rock audience leaving school in the eighties; dole, the black economy or some dead end job, it's not surprising a large percentage opted for life as a rock star.

They staggered round Rebels spouting attitude-charged rockisms

The fact that the 'rock star lifestyle' for most people in the 1980s was funded by a fortnightly dole cheque, embellished by a dodgy American accent with a distinct South Yorkshire twang and fuelled by Red Stripe (with the can filled with Safeway own brand gin) as they staggered round Rebels spouting attitude-charged rockisms, was neither here nor there.

The key to much of it, as it always was, was as much luck as it was talent.

When you start mulling over the Def Leppard success it's a small miracle they made it at all.

Their sound was the complete antithesis of what was going on in the UK – rock was dying and punk was king. But they definitely had what many fledgling bands lack – tenacity and self-belief.

If the line up at The Limit club's two day showcase of local talent was anything to go by they were going to need it – the majority of the city's bands were lining up to take the country by storm as part of Sheffield's celebrated electro movement.

Def Leppard were the only rock act on the bill, they were down to play the first day of the festival and they were supporting... Human League.

Pete Willis said: "I think it was Joe that had persuaded Kevan the owner to let us on the bill somewhere.

"We were slightly apprehensive about it because it appeared to be more punk and we were thinking it was going to be a bit hairy as everyone was going to be there to listen to electronic music.

"I remember it being a real shambles with three or four bands struggling about with equipment but it just ended up going down great.

"We did have a bit of 'rent a crowd' there to help us along but it ended up going down really good. It definitely surprised us."

Def Leppard took some stick in the early days – especially the flack they got for supposedly 'selling out' to America.There was probably more than a hint of jealousy.

Anyone that has ever been in a band knows they would give their right arm to sell an album, to anyone, anywhere...

At least someone was interested. The fact that the States were happy to buy millions was unbelievable.

It's a sad fact that bands that never hit the Def Leppard-esque big time are quickly forgotten so here's our rundown on some of the local acts that won't be initiated to Ohio's Rock And Roll Hall Of Fame some time soon but definitely deserve their place in Sheffield's own rock'n'roll hall of shame over the decades. Many of these bands are still very much in existence and you'll find a good percentage of them that are far more successful abroad than they are here in Blighty.

We've spread the net wide as has been the way with the growing numbers of sub-genres that have been content to sit under the rock banner.

We apologise in advance if we've forgotten anyone...

■ **ROADHOUSE:** critically acclaimed outfit formed by former Def Leppard guitarist Pete Willis. Released one self-titled album and toured with the likes of Ian Gillan. Line up included Paul Jackson on vocals and Richard Day on guitar. Legendary Sheffield rocker Pete Halliday was an early Roadhouse drummer

■ **GROOP DOGDRILL:** quality hard rocking act with a hint of punk and rockabilly that released two albums and a number of singles. Toured with everyone from Motorhead to a fledgling Hives. Should have been bigger

■ **DEATH TRASH:** storming Sheffield outfit who regularly disgraced the pages of the national music press in the late 1980s

■ **GYPSY TEASE:** Sheffield's contribution to glam

■ **FREEKSPURT:** will go down in history courtesy of generally unhinged front man Barry

■ **THE MIRIMAR DISASTER:** purveyors of cutting edge alternative metal that sadly split in 2008

■ **EDGE OF FAITH:** goth rockers that saw Mark 'DJ Mutley' Hobson try out a very short-lived career on vocals

■ **THE GRIND:** Corporation Keith's finest hour (he's also having a good times these days with The Fuckwits)

■ **HAZE:** very much of prog rock genre that kicked off in the seventies. They were formed in 1978 by Chirs and Paul McMahon. Their debut single was 'The Night'/'Dig Them Mushrooms'. Their first album, 'C'est La Vie' came out in 1984. Spent five years touring the country in an old ambulance. Recently played

30th anniversary shows in Sheffield and London. The brothers also appeared with a new band, World Turtle, in the early 1990s

■ **ETIQUETTE:** too many finest hours to mention but here goes... front man Johnny Loco signing autographs in the back of an ambulance after knocking himself out on stage at Sheffield City Hall. Getting lobbed out of Athena Sauna with Ice T and Bodycount after taking the LA thrash metalers on a night out in the city. Performing everywhere from Sheffield Arena to Birmingham NEC

■ **HERITAGE:** Sheffield/Rotherham metal band that supported Def Leppard as they rose through the ranks to greatness in the early 1980s. In 1981 they supported Witchfynde on tour. They released the 'Strange Place'/ 'Misunderstood' single in March 1981 and in 1983 had an album on Rondelet with a near completely different line up

■ **SPOILT BRATT:** Chesterfield-based glam marauders touted for greatness. Played an interesting gig at the John O' Gaunt in Gleadless with 'DJ Mark's Kiss Katz Mobile Disco' (Mark is now better known as metal overlord Mark 'DJ Mutley' Hobson who runs Corporation rock club in Sheffield). It was at that crazy time in the mid-eighties when every bar in the land found it necessary to have a 'rock night'

■ **GEDDES AXE:** touted as the next Def Leppard, they played regularly at Sheffield rock haunts like Wapentake Bar and The Broadfield and supported Saxon at Sheffield City Hall in 1980. The band were originally formed by Andy Barrott and Martin Wilson. Demos were cut quickly and these ended up topping various heavy metal charts at the time and led to very high profile gigs.

ETIQUETTE ON STAGE AT SHEFFIELD CITY HALL

Word spread to the ears of Geoff Barton of Sounds newspaper who did a big spread on them. They supported Def Leppard on their first tour and headlined the Marquee in London a few times. Andy Barrott left and joined Heritage before moving to Bradford and joining Baby Tuckoo. He returned to Sheffield and played with the Lonely Hearts in the 1980s.

■ **ALIBI:** rock band that started as early as 1976 and split in 1981

■ **CAIRO:** formed in 1982 and featuring original Def Leppard drummer Tony Kenning along with singer and guitarist Gerry Fletcher (who later became an actor on Emmerdale). They recorded 'Eight Bells'/'Inside Out' on August 1984.

■ **SARACEN:** enduring rockers from nearby Matlock who released the notable 'Heroes, Saints & Fools' album in the heady days of 1981 and continue the fight up to this day

■ **MONROE** (later renamed Torrcha): fine metal mayhem in the days when vertical hair was as important than the music. All was fine and dandy until a gig at Sheffield Poly when Saxon, who were in

SPOILT BRATT

MONROE (LATER TO BECOME TORRCHA) WITH FRIENDS

TORRCHA

the audience, decided to poach the band's drummer Nigel Durham

■ **STRONGHEART:** probably a band that proved Sheffield's metal credentials once and for all. Why else would they form in glam capital of the universe, Los Angeles, and then relocate the Steel City? Get in! Strongheart were formed in the City of Angels in 1988 by Wilbur & Bobby with Bill Evans on bass. They moved to the City of Devil Signs soon after and built a sizeable following and even entertained the metal masses at Roxys Rock Night

■ **AMNESIA:** finest thrash metal from Steel City

■ **PEARL HARBOUR:** hats off to this lot for persuading Coronation Street star Reg Holdsworth, who was massive at the time, to be the star of their promo video. The band comprised former Spoilt Bratt guitarist Rick Anderson, ex-Angel Train drummer Phil Sturmer and bassist Craig Buttery who failed a Hanoi Rocks audition for being too pissed to play

PEARL HARBOUR

■ **BITTER SUITE/PHIL BRODIE BAND:** enduring Sheffield act that opened the city's renowned Limit venue in 1978, have appeared in a number of guises over the years and still gig today. A long and impressive career has seen them tour worldwide and performed everywhere from Rock City to Berlin Olympic Stadium

■ **MEL AND NEIL GABBITAS.** Local rock legends who've popped up in bands (separately) spanning Chinawhite to Tracy Hunter (daughter of Ian Hunter) over the years

■ **PHIL 'PHILTHY ANIMAL' TAYLOR:** Chesterfield-born Motorhead drummer

■ **KIK:** Kerrang! Radio faves fronted by the enigmatic D'Lear. Great image and memorable industrial rock slices like 'Crack Whore Barbi'. Band member Presley also has a nice sideline temping for Gary Numan

■ **UBERBYTE:** Fine industrial noise merchants making a serious dent on the scene

■ **REPROBATE:** formed in Sheffield in the early 1990s playing with the likes of Pestilence and Skyclad. Split and then reformed in 2008. Ones to watch. Recently voted best unsigned band by readers of Terrorizer magazine

■ **BAL SAGOTH:** epic black metal band that originally formed in 1993. Released numerous albums and a major force to be reckoned with, especially overseas. They recently performed at the charmingly titled Brutal Assault festival in the Czech Republic and headlined another you should take the parents to next year, the Heathen Crusade II festival in Minnesota

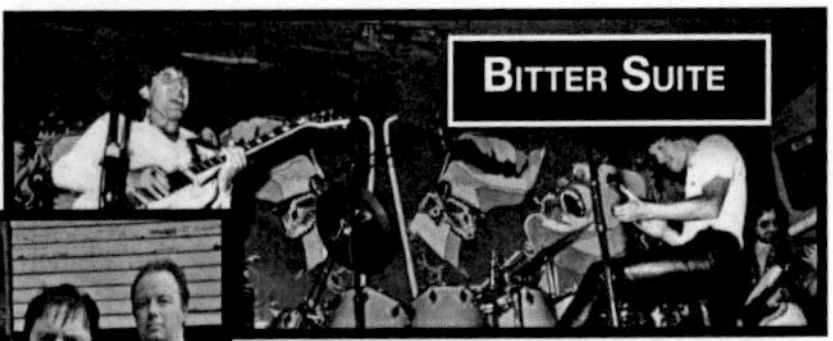
BITTER SUITE

■ **TARA'S SECRET:** another Sheffield act making a big noise abroad and worth looking out for. Released their third album, Vertigo, last year. Recent claims to fame include being crowned 'Band of the Month' in Argentina and described as a 'melodic monster' in Greece

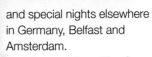

TARA'S SECRET

■ **LEATHER ZOO:** highly successful rock/punk band that have toured Europe extensively and headlined Berlin's Volkspark Football Stadium in front of 15,000

■ **ZAYUS:** first outing for Sheffield drummer Pete Halliday. Regular appearances at The Penguin in Shiregreen and did a live spot for Colin Slade on Radio Hallam

■ **Siiiii:** These major hitting goth rockers were originally formed in 1983 and played with the likes of Skeletal Family and March Violets in the first phase of the goth scene. They split in 1985 and everyone thought that was it until email correspondence in 2005 between singer Paul Devine and rock journalist Mick Mercer persuaded them to regroup. They've already performed at the Drop Dead Festival in New York, The Gothic Pogo Festival in Leipzig and special nights elsewhere in Germany, Belfast and Amsterdam.

Siiiii IN THE 1980s

REPROBATE BACK IN THE DAY

And then not forgetting (in no particular order) Nightrun, The Absolute, Thunderchilde, Midnight Choir, AC Temple, The Bride Wore Black, Personality Crisis, StoneRun, Cleopatra, Stateline,Cincinatti, Scream The Rose, Count Dante, Various Vegetables, Havana Rocks, Blameless, Tiananmen, Jurys Out, Cruel Device, Sweet Cyanide, Silverjet, Sanctuary, Tikkaboo Peak, Deadline, SWON, Wicked, Elfin, Bhuna, UV-Pop, Area 52, Mike TV, The Flight Commander, Renegade, Tokyo, Bullrush, Fights, Fine (who became Redder), Hoggboy (now The Hosts), Ill-Logic, Trolleydogshag (including Steve Mackey from Pulp), and Fixer.

And finally... Elephant Key, (Sub Nova), Mae's Lost Empire, Downslide, Two Gun, Laruso, Tuscany Fruit Bats, In The Name Of, Catharsis Collapse, Angel Train, Head Up, Disarm, Roxberg, Smoke, FC Dog, Durban, Tarana, Dead By Friday, Cry, Crimes of Passion, Wolfman Circus, Treebeard, CRF, Lyca Sleep, Blitz, Deadline, Stress Baby, Whisky Haze, Double Eclipse, Fiendish, CRF, Von Daniken, GGF, Fuck City Shitters, Left Ajar, Black Mariah, Baby Tuckoo, Dedringer, Sparta, Tokyo Rose, Phoenix Rising, Secret Noise, Treacle, Val Halla, Diva, Schaiffer, Drowning Not Waving, Last Chance and Candy Paige.

PANZA DIVISION: a band whose posters seemingly adorned every available piece of fly posting space in the early eighties. Released 'We'll Rock The World' single in 1982 and generally finely regarded. Featuring vocalist/guitarist Glenn Marples, Rick Corcoran, vocals/guitar, Andy 'Spider' Freestone, drums, Alan Edwards, bass, and Eugene Reynolds, drums. Glenn Marples originally formed Rokka releasing one single and toured with Sheffield sixties star Dave Berry – a man cited in the seventies as the 'godfather of punk'.

Panza Division were very much on the cusp of the British New Wave Of Heavy Metal and should have been far bigger. They played with everyone from Saxon to Girl via Twisted Sister.

In 1983 they changed their name to Lonely Hearts and toured the States as well as extensive shows in the UK.

Their most bizarre show was in 1990 on Emmerdale Farm – the start and finish of Glenn's acting career.

These days Glenn resides in Ibiza and still rocks for Britain. Good on him!

Glenn Marples said: "I think we met as the band Rokka in the Penthouse and we certainly did our first gig there as Panza. We got the name from a competition on Colin Slade's Radio Hallam rock show it is from the title of a song by the band Budgie. Colin's show was how most local rock bands got their first radio interview and demo play and we got paid. The late Dave Kilner used to set up the studio gear and make us coffee. We wrote and recorded the theme tune 'Rock Show Blowout' which is still used today - I know because I get the odd 5 quid in royaties ha ha. We toured the UK playing in pubs and the then vast Working Mens Club circuit A.K.A the entertainers graveyard, but the best way to learn the craft. I remember one of our first gigs outside Sheffield was at Leeds Fforde Green a gig all the best rock bands were playing then. It was in a dodgy area of Leeds and notorious as a chicken wire gig. In the dressing room someone had drawn an arrow on the wall pointing to the stage and underneath written 'TO THE LIONS',

"I shit myself, but we had some great nights there. The onstage interruptions were famous, one night the police came in and insisted on using our PA to play the Yorkshire Ripper Tape - try and win the crowd after that!

"Another time they stopped us playing in the middle of a ripping guitar solo

Drummer 'Bubbles' dies

A MUSICIAN who put the beat into many of Sheffield's popular live bands has died of a heart attack.

Drummer Steve 'Bubbles' Mitchell was only in his mid-50s and had not long rejoined some of his old pals to play in local band Charlie Don't Surf.

The much-liked music man, who was a painter and decorator by trade, began earning his reputation in the mid '60s.

Initially calling himself Steve Moon, a reference to his hero, the tragic Who drummer Keith Moon, Steve started out with the Bob Davis Mood.

His curly hair earned him the nickname Bubbles as he went on to play with one of Sheffield's better-known acts Bitter Suite. Rock bands Lonely Hearts, Panza Division, blues man Frank White and country outfit Big Sky all employed Steve's talents.

Three times married and a father, he moved to Doncaster in the early '90s, but recently began playing on his former stomping ground.

Steve died of a heart attack on December 30 at his home in Bessacarr, Doncaster. His funeral service, on Wednesday at City Road (2.15pm), will be followed by a gathering at Woodhouse West End Club.

Any donations can be made to the Martin House Children's Hospital, in Wetherby, where one of Steve's children was treated.

Andy Fisher, of Charlie Don't Surf, had played with Steve in previous bands.

"He touched so many people that he met. He was always so funny to be around. And he was always a superb drummer."

Phil Brodie, formerly guitarist of Bitter Suite and still a popular draw on the live circuit with his own band, said Steve could have played at a higher level.

"He was just brilliant. He was like Simon Kirke of Free and could easily have played with a band of that calibre."

Brilliant: Steve 'Bubbles' Mitchell

to ask me "ah tha registered for VAT?"."We were always contracted and they timed it to the second, then they would ask us to do one more song, eventually I got fed up with this and said look if your boss asks you to work over you want some more dosh right - he said 'yeah', I said 'so do we', 'ah much does tha want', so I said 'how about a round of drinks', 'allreet' he says. SO I had someone build me a clocking in machine and at the start of the show we clocked in and at the end clocked out it would then flash OVERTIME OVERTIME we would play 3 encores and get loads more dosh, as did all the bands on the circuit after that. In 82 (I think) we won best rock band in The Star/ Websters South Yorkshire band contest, this got us on to the university and large hall circuit together with the radio play and press reviews we were getting.

National Coaches had a promotion with Mars bars and you got a token with each bar save enough and you got a free ride to the smoke... the band lived on Mars bars for 2 months. We had to change the name in the end because when we went to London they turned up expecting neo Nazis, skinheads would come with NF tattooed on their foreheads, wankers. The last straw was at Rotherham motor show with The Specials and a riot broke out.

"The night before we flew to the States, Rick and I had the best idea ever, ever, lets stay up all night, and we did until about 30 mins before we should have woken up.

"We missed the bus for London and tried to call a cab.

SOLID Entertainments

5, BARGATE, GRIMSBY, SOUTH HUMBERSIDE. DN34 4SS. TEL. (0472) 41031

"SOLID ROCK ONE"

LEEDS Queens Hall Saturday 28th May '83

RUNNING ORDER TO BE STRICTLY ADHERED TO

ACT	ON STAGE TIME	MUST BE OFF BY	TOTAL PLAYING TIME INC. ENCORE S
PANZA DIVISION	1.55 (Change over 15 mins	2.15	20 mins
BATTLE AXE	2.30 (Change over 15 mins)	2.50	20 mins
PICTURE	3.05 (Change over 15 mins)	3.35	30 mins
SPIDER	3.50 (change over 20 mins)	4.20	30 mins
ANVIL	4.40 (change over 30 mins)	5.25	45 mins
GIRLSCHOOL	5.55 (change over 30 mins)	6.45	50 mins
TWISTED SISTER	7.15 (change over 45 mins)	8.15	1 hour
SAXON	9.00	10.30pm	1½ hours

"NODDY HOLDER" FROM SLADE will introduce each act.
DOORS OPEN 12 noon

"In living memory no one had taken a cab to London (rich people took the fast train or flew) so they would not believe us. Anyway eventually we managed to get a cabbie to come and look at our money and so for a hefty sum plus a bonus if we made it on time we hit the M1 at warp speed. I fell asleep listening to the monotone voice of the girl in the taxi office saying 'Wybourn anybody Wybourn,Wybourn anybody Wybourn.' The Emmerdale thing was a call from the agent who booked artists for Y.T.V. I think he had seen our video for 'Wild Wind Blows' on MTV. I thought it was a wind up at first and the band did all the way to the location."

GOGMAGOG: Definitely not wholly South Yorkshire but worth a nod for being one of the most bizarre spin-offs of the rock scene from the 1980s metalmania and one of the future projects undertaken by original Def Leppard guitarist Pete Willis.

Jonathan King invited him to join the British supergroup that featured former Iron Maiden members Paul Di'Anno and Clive Burr, former White Spirit and Gillan guitarist Janick Gers (himself a then future member of Iron Maiden) and bassist Neil Murray, who has played in over 30 bands, including Whitesnake, Black Sabbath, and John Sloman's Badlands.

Pete Willis said: "It was more out of curiosity that I got involved. He sent me this tape with three rough ideas for songs that had been written by a guy called Russ Ballard and some literature with it about Gogmagog and the devil rising or something . I thought, 'is it going to be like some death metal band or something?'"

"I went down for a meeting at a hotel and there was singer Paul Di'Anno and Janick Gers and, surprisingly enough, John Entwhilstle and Cozy Powell!"

The two latter names didn't appear at any other meetings but everyone else was intrigued enough to see the project through to its end – which Pete is the first to admit wasn't a massive drain on his time and looked as though Jonathan King was more interested in setting a new world record for rock track recording techniques.

"He said we'd have to get together quickly to record these tracks and quickly was definitely the operative word. He sent me this itinerary said 'meet 9am, pre-production until 10.30am' which gave me enough time to have a cup of tea, a bacon sandwich and tune my guitar!"

In essence they had time to run through the song once.

"The next part of the itinerary said 'lunch' and then 'into the studio from 1.30pm until 4.30pm'. I thought 'crikey'. I ended up adding my own bit to the end which said '4.30pm to 6.30pm' American tour!"

The evening was more relaxed. "He took us all out for a nice meal", Pete Willis said "and that was about the last I heard of it really."

All that was ever released of this officially was the three-song 'I Will Be There' EP in 1985. It was all a far cry from King's original idea which was to form a heavy metal band a write a rock opera.

Pete Willis said: ""It was a good laugh doing it but it was all over in a flash."

PLAYING SCRABBLE WITH ZEPPELIN'S GOTHFATHER

SIMON HINKLER

Simon Hinkler was arguably one of the city's best known and successful rock musicians of the late eighties/early nineties. The multi-instrumentalist and former member of city-based acts including Artery and Midnight Choir joined probably the most high-profile goth band of their generation, The Mission. The Mission gig actually came via Simon Hinkler's production of an album by Sheffield punk band Mau Maus at Fairview Studio in Hull.

He said: "The engineer there told me that Gary Marx (Sisters of Mercy guitarist) had secretly been in there last week demoing some songs and was about to quit the Sisters.

"I casually said, 'well if they need another guitarist tell them to give me a call'. About 9 months past and it was all long forgotten. Then one day I got a call from Wayne (Hussey) who had just split from the Sisters, and had been given my number. I went up to Leeds on the bus, and met with Wayne, Craig and Mick. Then a few days later went back up again for auditions. They auditioned about a dozen guitarists and they said I'd blown away the competition...which was nice."

Many have debated the whole rock v goth tag over the years. The Mission firmly nailed their rock credentials to the mast by enlisting the help of one John Paul Jones on production duties.

Simon Hinkler said: "Goth's a tag that was acquired by – thrust upon - several quite different bands in the '80s. However, the generation that followed narrowed it right down to a caricature. Wayne (Hussey) was quite happy to court the goth tag (his philosophy was that all publicity is good publicity) whereas the rest of us wanted to keep it more in an alternative rock vein. I think that's where it went wrong really, because we were a great live rock band, but acquired the tag and alienated most of the wider rock audience.

"In the late '80s there were a few bands that were compared with Led Zeppelin, including ourselves and some of the poofy soft metal bands like Whitesnake. Both Robert Plant and John Paul Jones went on record as saying that they liked The Mission and thought we were original, whereas the others weren't.

"When we came to do our second album we had a short list of possible producers including Eno, Kate Bush, and John Paul Jones. Fully aware of how it would set the tongues wagging we went with JP. We spent 14 weeks locked away with him at The Manor and The Townhouse. He was a thoroughly nice chap. We had experienced whirlwind success and insane excesses on tours; JP basically stepped in and calmed us all right down. We nicknamed him the Gothfather. I spent hours playing Scrabble with him...he's pretty good.

"So much happened over a period of five years, and a lot of it becomes a blur of hotels, airports and dressing rooms, but high spots would have to include playing Sheffield City Hall with all my family there. There were so many great gigs...Lorelei Festival in Germany is a top day out. Headlining Reading twice. We sold out Wembley Arena and the Birmingham NEC at the height of it all; with live broadcast on Radio One.

"Anecdotes? There are so many! Here's a good tour story: The morning after a US show our tour manager goes to the hotel reception to settle up, saying "...and there's been some damage done to a wardrobe which we'll pay for. The desk clerk says "no problem we'll just take a look and assess the cost. Which room is it in?" Tour manager replies, "well actually it's in a tree outside."

Though Simon's wardrobe is more at home on his bedroom floor these days he's set to be back in action this year.

FROM SKULLCRUSHER TO SWAMPWALK

Gary Holmes and his renowned Skullcrusher fanzine acted as the underground mouthpiece for much of the region's metal scene in the early eighties. His work deserves major recognition.
He was producing the fanzine on a weekly basis for a full year with most of the copies being sold to Wapentake regulars.

Copies of the now ultra-rare magazine read like a who's who of the generation of local rock bands that sprung up in the wake of the early success of Def Leppard. The ultimate prize – at that point at least - was landing a session with Radio Hallam's Colin Slade on his revered rock show.

Panza Division, Geddes Axe, Bitter Suite, Fallen Angel, Asphyxia, Amulet, Alyx , Graffiti, Madison Blooze, Whammer Jammer, Tokyo, Vortex, Prisoner (Bitter Suite off-shoot) and Haze were just a few of the bands that regularly featured as well as gigs at venues like The Penguin, Marples, Sheffield Polytechnic, Sheffield University, Rotherham Arts Centre, Maltby's Queens Hotel, Chesterfield's Brimington Tavern and many others.

DJ Ken would compile his own Wapentake chart; there'd be a heavy metal crossword and things would be interspersed with ads for Keith Bradley's Heavy Rock Roadshow at Hemsworth's John 'O' Gaunt every Wednesday.

Gary Holmes, as things were in the early eighties for many people, had to keep a low profile. He was signing on and went under the moniker 'Gary Kowalski'.

His success with Skullcrusher led him to put together the now legendary 'Steel City Rock' compilation cassette which showcased many of the key acts from that era. It included the likes of Alyx, Black Mariah, Chinawhite, Fallen Angel, Renegade and Storm.

Gary Holmes' own musical career is most noted for his success with the renowned Swampwalk in the 1990s. The critically acclaimed act, which included Andy Barrott – former guitarist with Geddes Axe, Chrome Molly and Baby Tuckoo – were regulars in Kerrang! and narrowly missed out on the publication's coveted 'single of the week' to Pantera.

They notched up two albums – 'Strangled at Birth' and 'Technicolour Vomit Jet' – and were signed to Bleeding Hearts Records. They are well worth a listen.
Think Wildhearts turned up to eleven.

SWAMPWALK

Seventh Son

Sheffield's own Pulp proved it's worth having staying power. They formed in the late 1970s and didn't hit major commercial success until the 1990s.

Seventh Son are definitely one of the most enduring rock bands in the country and if staying power equated to commercial success – well they'd eat Pulp for breakfast. First formed in Barnsley in 1980, they fully deserve their place in Malc Macmillan's 'The New Wave of British Heavy Metal Encyclopaedia'. Their passion and perseverance has kept them going through four decades of ups and downs.

Brothers Kev and Bri O'Shaughnessy first formed the band. They landed a coveted session on Colin Slade's Radio Hallam rock show a couple of years later.

Forty years and many musicians later and the band are still going strong.

Seventh Son are still a cornerstone of the region's metal community.

These days they're signed to German label Metal Pages with the line-up of Bri, Rick Gregory, Dave Fox and Kev Lee. You'll also find Bri providing his esteemed vocal services to Oliver/Dawson Saxon.

Seventh Son

Panza Division perform at the Sheffield Show in 1978

Sheffield's All-conquering Bring Me The Horizon in 2010

BLACK SPIDERS

Formed in 2008, this hard rocking outfit tore through the metal music industry like a tsunami before calling it a day in 2017. They performed at Download within months of forming and were quickly labelled as hot property within the music press. Support slots with acts spanning Ozzy to Airbourne soon arrived and they were named 'Best Underground Band' by Metal Hammer in 2010. Their debut 'Sons of the North' album had major acclaim.

More success, music and a follow up 'This Savage Land' ground to a halt when they split in 2017. They've now reformed. Get ready.

WHILE SHE SLEEPS

Originating from Renishaw, this rising force in the metalcore world first formed in 2006. They received the Best British Newcomer awards at the Kerrang! Awards in 2012. The band have worked tirelessly since the early days and held a launch show for their first album at Sheffield's Plug nightclub in 2010. They've enjoyed a close relationship with with fellow city rockers Bring Me The Horizon and made massive in-roads in the States.

Album number five, 'Sleeps Society', is set for release in 2021.

DUKES OF BORDELLO

DUKES OF BORDELLO

High octane rock'n'roll trio that have making an addictive racket for the past six years or so. Relentless gigging, song writing and mayhem means they'll soon have clocked up their third album. Led by Andy Barrott, a true elder statesman of Sheffield metal, the Dukes of Bordello offer a searing live show and enviable back catalogue. In the words of the band... 'This is pure snot nosed rebellious rock'n'roll with its middle finger pointing firmly in the air."

More Memories

Mark Lindley

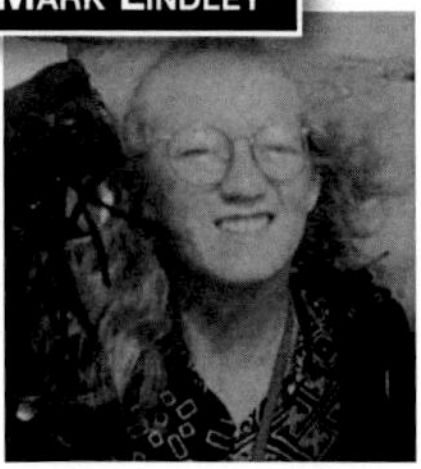

Mark Lindley has fond memories of nights at Sheffield's rock clubs in the late 1980s.

"From mid-1988 to 1992 my fave attire when going to Rebels was a vest top or, if it was a hot summer night, a waistcoat with bare chest! Or maybe a silk shirt with all the bangles up both arms and a Bon Jovi 'Slippery When Wet' pendant; very tight ripped jeans or my stars 'n' stripes candy striped jeans (loved 'em) cowboy boots or hi tops (boots for definite if attending Roxys Rock nite). Now my hair which was blonde was blow-dried whilst I hung upside down over the landing. Then I used my three cans of hard rock hair spray to get the desired look (always had a spare can in my jeans pocket which looked very... well...). At the same time sipping a copious amount of Jack 'n' coke before getting the 76 bus from Sheffield Lane Top into town for the first stop which was the Wap, then onto Yorkie (summer had to be the Yorkie beer back yard) then back to the Wap and back to Yorkie before running the gauntlet through town before arriving at Rebels for rock'n'roll heaven."

Rebels - rock music's own Wigan Casino

John Stabler says you can never underestimate the influence Rebels rock club had in helping introduce the rock audience to new artists. He said: "It was through Rebels, DJ Bob Maltby and the odd rock journalist that many of us came across more obscure, non-commercial bands in the early to mid '80s. Chart success for the likes of Whitesnake, Def Leppard, Motörhead etc, was great for rock in general, but some amazing bands emerged through the early '80s who had little or no chart success and certainly no sort of commercial or media exposure. So these bands became huge names on the rock scene thanks to Rebels. Shades record store London was a main source for albums reviewed in the likes of Kerrang! and many of us bought vinyl and tapes having never heard these albums before. Enter Rebels and Bob Maltby.

They would accommodate club goers by playing tracks off the tapes we'd brought in.

Through this, Bob himself would get hold of albums from the likes of White Sister, Orion, Dokken, Stone Fury, White Lion, FM, Bonfire and many others with no radio exposure, apart from the odd track on Tommy Vance's Friday Rock show. They were now building cult followings. I remember going to see FM supported by White Sister in Sheffield and talking to the WS band members after their set. They were blown away at the audience reaction and the fact we knew all the lyrics to their songs. The part Rebels and Bob played in this should never be underestimated. For me Rebels was the rock version of northern soul's Wigan Casino – it became the place to hear tracks from so many bands previously unheard of. These are albums I still play today.

Walking up those many steps and hearing Dokken's 'In My Dreams' blasting out of Bob's speakers the second you were in ear shot. What a way to start the weekend. Great times, brilliant club. Good memories."

Bob Maltby - The DJ that provided the sounds for a rock generation

Bob Maltby (left) with Lez Wright (former Rebels DJ) and the Bailey Brothers at the launch party for the original 'Signing On For The Devil.'

Bob Maltby was one of Sheffield's earliest rock DJs. He started at the Penthouse and carved out a name for himself in the early years of Rebels. He said:

"It all began way back in about 1977/1978, I was a customer in the Penthouse and became friends with the DJ who was called Dave May, his mother worked in the cloakroom and sold the ciggies (lovely woman), I'm not sure how it came about but Dave left and they were stuck for a DJ. The manager at the time was Alan Slingsby and I said I would do it. He asked if I'd done it before and I said yes. I hadn't of course but I went up on the stage and muddled my way through.

I continued to spin the discs right up until the Penthouse closed.

I twiddled my thumbs for sometime afterwards, wondering what to do next, when I got a call from Dave May asking if I would stand in for him on the coming Sunday night at the Saddle on West Street. I agreed and for some reason Dave never came back, so I carried on starting with just the Sunday night which became very busy. As a result of that I ended up doing four nights a week. Thankfully my girlfriend at the time (Rosanna) had bought me some double decks on the never never. They were very happy times in the Saddle at the end of the seventies and start of the eighties

At the same time there was a place called the KGB that was in the dance hall part of the Abbeydale Cinema and was doing rock discos on Friday and Saturday night. Living just up the road I used to frequent the place and there were always people telling me that I should be djing there, but the two fellas running it were not keen. I think it was a mate of theirs that was djing at the time. Anyway, after a while and some pressure from the punters they decided to give me a chance. They obviously thought I wouldn't be any good and, because there weren't that many people going in, they agreed to pay me 25p per head. They thought they were onto a good thing! However, on the first night the place was packed and they had to pay me a fortune - needless to say they decided to pay me a set fee per night after that. I ended up filling Saturdays nights for some months. Then a lad I knew from the Penthouse helped persuade Steve Baxendale – who was about to open Rebels – that he should use me for the a Friday night. I played the first rock night at Rebels. When I went to the KGB on the Saturday I was fired on the spot. Steve heard about this and, because the first night was so successful, he agreed to let me do Saturdays at Rebels as well. I continued to DJ at the club until 1990 when, after an argument about a particular track, I promptly turned the music off and walked out and that was my last night. The management, a chap called Ron, was into soul music and said I wasn't allowed to play thrash metal. He came up on the stage and started telling me what I should be playing and that was it.

Rebels was originally going to a reggae bar, but as Steve said, the rockers drank gallons of Newcastle Brown and beer and lager as opposed the reggae crowd that made a Britvic orange last all night.

Music has always been a big thing in my family. My mother was only 17 when she had me so was still very young while I was growing up. We listened to all the usual things Radio 1, Pick of the Pops and of course Top of the Pops and we always had a record player. My mum would play all the hits of time

The early days of Rebels were amazing - the doors opened at 8pm and closed at 2am and at the weekend people queued all the way up the Haymarket and by 8.15 we were packed all night. Luckily the sound system at Rebels was amazing and very loud, you could hear the music as soon as you turned down the Haymarket.

A lot of very special friendships were made at Rebels and most people from those wonderful days meet up regularly. Most of them are on Facebook, just like me looking that bit older but perhaps not that much wiser - lol.

As for the contribution that South Yorkshire made, well we had Def Leppard and Saxon as well of others that were very successful over the eighties. One of my very small claims to fame is related to Def Leppard. They'd not gone to America at that point and had produced 1000 copies of their first single. They gave me a copy and at the time I was doing a rock chart for Sounds music paper on a weekly basis. Basically it was the top ten tracks that were popular that week in Rebels. John Peel, I think it was, had played the Def Leppard single on Radio One and people had heard it, liked it and noticed that it was also mentioned in my weekly rock charts. I received loads of letters, some of which I still have, asking me where they could buy the single from.

Most nights in Rebels were very similar. It was mostly the same people - so much so that it was one of those places that if you went out on your own and came to Rebels later, you would always find a friend. It was such a special place and everyone has some fantastic memories. The police were very happy with the Rebels crowd as it was the most peaceful night club in Sheffield regarding trouble, this was left to the suit and tie brigade that went to Roxy's and place like that.

We had a few rock stars come in Rebels after playing the City Hall, mostly the support bands but occasionally some big names. One night Lemmy and Motörhead came in and caused quite a stir. Something occurred with the bouncers that night and Lemmy and crew left and smashed up their cars parked on Dixon Lane.

"You couldn't be a fashion band up north - you had to deliver on the night."
Graham Oliver

It would be difficult to say what my favourite song would be as I liked just about everything I played. Perhaps that was partly why Rebels was so good, I was enjoying myself so much that it fed into the crowd. I'd have to say that Magic Power by Triumph is a great favourite, thinking about it now, In the Still of the Night by Whitesnake is probably one of my favourite songs especially when played on the Rebels amazing sound system. I remember that the bass bins on the sound system were huge and we often found people asleep in them - I can't imagine what their head was like the next day, but I'm glad it wasn't mine. The sound system was a custom affair built by someone Steve Baxendale knew and I've never heard better since.

Taxi drivers that liked rock music used sit on Haymarket and listen to the music in between fares.

To the best of my memory there were about 90 stairs up to Rebels, certainly there was nine flights of stairs and I think nine or 10 steps on each flight. The Rebels crowd thought they were steep, but try carrying thousands of records up to the top every night (in the early days) and just remember that all the beer and stuff was carried to the top. In fact at Christmas Rebels bought extra stocks of beer and lager etc and on top of carrying it up the Rebels stairs they then had to lift it onto the roof for storage."

STEEL CITY ROCKERS IN ACTION

MARGE AND OLGA

Chapter 11

TEN YEARS LATER - GONE BUT NOT FORGOTTEN

Nearly a year into a global pandemic and a sweaty moshpit is as about as far removed from our socially distanced world of 2020 than you could ever get.

The music and entertainment industry has undoubtably been one of the hardest hit.

But we thought we'd leave it up to the Bailey Brothers to wrap up the last ten years since the first edition of this book with a nod to some of the national and international stars that were part of their orbit and are sadly no longer with us:

"What a decade it has been since the original 'Signing On For The Devil'. We have lost many friends in the business who have brought so much pleasure to thousands of fans worldwide. We'd like to pay our respects to a few:

IAN FRASER KILMISTER, KNOWN TO US ALL AS LEMMY:

We first met Lemmy and Motörhead on the 'Ace of Spades' tour in Leeds, without a doubt they were one of the loudest rock bands we've ever heard. He was one of the first to offer a welcoming hand of friendship when the Bailey Brothers secured a residency in Hammersmith, London.

The MTV interview we did with Lemmy, Fast Eddie Clarke and Lea Heart was one

WITH LEMMY

With members of Fastway and Saxon at Radio Hallam

of our favourites. Lemmy insisted we met in the pub next door to our studio. Several Jack Daniels later we are on set and he still wants to drink, so we all ended up filling plastic cups and drinking during the interview. The biggest laugh was when Lemmy and Eddie took about 40 minutes to do us a 10 second show trailer. Eddie was in stitches, in fact all the studio crew were crying tears of laughter, they were hilarious. Lemmy was extremely intelligent and very well read. You always thought he was indestructible so his death was very upsetting. We miss Lemmy; his passing left a huger crater in the rock n roll landscape.

Phil 'Philthy Animal' Taylor - drummer – Motörhead:

We always like to see local musicians achieve great heights; he was born in Hasland, Chesterfield, and was the engine driving the classic Motorhead three-piece juggernaut. He actually died the month before Lemmy which was a sad year for all Motörhead fans.

Fast Eddie Clarke - guitarist/ songwriter - Motörhead & Fastway:

And then there were none! That's right, the original classic Motörhead line up was no more. Fast Eddie, although famed for being in Motörhead, also showed a more melodic edge to his writing and guitar playing. Fast Eddie Clarke formed Fastway in 1983 with famed UFO bass player Pete Way, hence the name Fastway. However, Pete never played on their self-titled Fastway debut album as he left and formed Waysted.
We can remember getting involved with

selecting some bands to play down at Dingwalls in Sheffield. Fastway was one of them, also Magnum, Limelight, Geddes Axe, Girlschool, Blackfoot Sue and many more. The six regional Dingwalls venues didn't last long but it was fun having one in Sheffield. Eddie Clarke, Lea Hart, (Fastway) Graham Oliver and Steve Dawson (Ex Saxon) all joined us in Sheffield for The Bailey Brothers Rock Show which was a networked radio show. Always had a laugh with Eddie Clarke but as previously mentioned, that day we spent together hanging with him and Lemmy before and after the interview, remains a lasting memory.

PETE WAY:

Oh my, this one hurt. Pete Way was a legend of the rock world, he set the bar in terms of stage presence - who didn't want a pair of black and white striped trousers after seeing him don them? His Gibson Thunderbird bass guitar hanging so low, he would be all over the stage. That classic UFO line up of Parker, Way, Mogg, Raymond and Schenker wrote and performed some of the best melodic hard rock of any decade. UFO were also legends of the rock'n'roll party life style.

We first met Pete Way in 1977, just two UFO fans with our mates from Sheffield following the band from city to city. We met the band back stage in Birmingham, Newark, then on the third consecutive day, Blackpool. Our Union Jack with Sheffield across it was recognisable to all instantly.

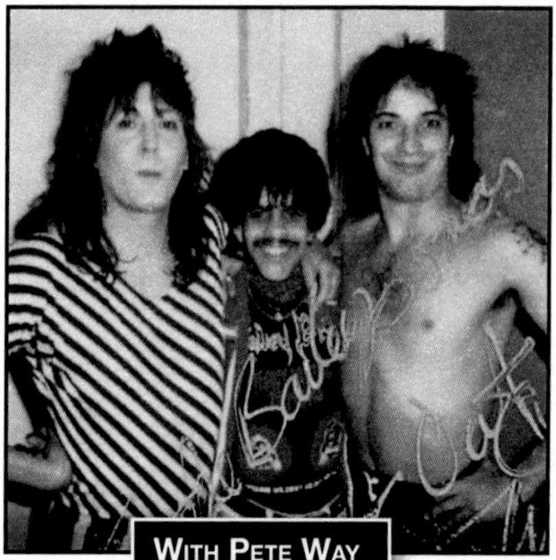

WITH PETE WAY

Pete was so friendly to us in Blackpool, he couldn't believe the support and told his tour manager to make us guests for the rest of the tour. That tour for us was not without incident however. After the Newark gig we were singing in the streets in the early hours; it was the Silver Jubilee and we were in good spirits. The locals complained and the next thing we are getting chased by the police. Without getting all BLM or political, Mick and I were forever getting harassed by the police, but seriously - chased around Newark for singing? To cut to the chase we just let them catch us but not Mick, he was like a greyhound back then. He hid in a dust bin like cartoon character 'Top Cat'! We were held there till almost daylight when eventually Mick walked in 'cos he was bored. They let us go in the morning and we then drove to Blackpool.

After the Blackpool show, a French girl and friends invited us back to her flat to hang out. We had only been there an hour when a knock on the door turned into a huge argument between her and her landlord. Before you could say deja vous, the police came, went straight for the Baileys, pushed us into a van then took us to a police cell. They kept us for hours until I pulled out the tour guest pass and told them we were with UFO and needed to be traveling to our next show. I said our lawyer will be getting a call if you don't let us out. Eventually we were released, obviously without charge. Talk about if your faces don't fit.

Love UFO and met Pete quite a few times over the years, in fact we nearly did a project together. He will be missed by so many - a lovely bloke.

Steve Lee:

The first band we had contact with from Switzerland was Krokus. We worked with them at Retford Porter House in about 1980/81. Roll on a few decades and the incredible Gotthard won the hearts of fans worldwide. We always got on really well with the band. Our last meeting was an invite to hang at one of our favourite local venues, the Corporation. It was tragic what happened to Steve, he was a lovely guy and amazing front man and vocalist.

With Gary Moore

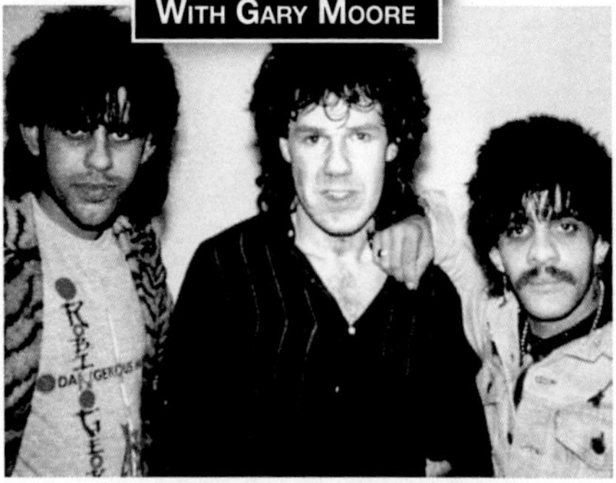

Gary Moore:

Mick introduced him as Mr Gary Guitar Moore when we interviewed him for our MTV show. He was a brilliant guitar player with songs such as 'Empty Rooms', 'Out In The Fields', 'Parisienne Walkways', 'The Loner' bringing back memories. Nobody did those Celtic driven anthems better than Gary. 'Over The Hills And Far Away' a good example from 1987 from the 'Wild Frontiers' album.

1990 saw a change in direction from hard rock to blues. He sort of enjoyed two bites of the cherry because his blues albums were a major success. 'Still Got The Blues' is an example of his ability as both a composer and performer. He played every note live like his life depended on it. We reviewed a live show he did at the Sheffield City Hall for Metal Hammer magazine. He would always receive a warm welcome there. The City Hall is one of our favourite venues.

Jan Kuehnemund:

A nod to those beautiful women in rock. Having gigged with Girlschool and Rock Goddess back in the day, we knew all girl bands could hold their own in the male dominated rock world. We had a memorable time with Vixen in Holland, interviewing them for TV and then watching them live at the Paradiso venue.

WITH BLACK SABBATH

WITH LEE GOTTHARD

VIXEN AND BAILEYS ON THE SET OF MTV

Jan was a stunning looking woman and a really good lead guitar player. Don't ever get fooled by image, this was no lipstick and leather act thrown together for eye candy. Roxy we already knew from meeting her back in 1985 when she was in Madam X. She's a kick ass drummer, Share on bass also plays with Joe Elliot's Down 'n' Outz side project away from Def Leppard. She's a very talented bass player. Janet Gardner is also a great vocalist so you had some major talent in Vixen and they were a tight live band.

DAVID BOWIE:

"There's a star man calling you at home. He'd like to come and meet us but you put down the bloody phone"

There are rock legends and then there's David Bowie. So I get a call from Mick: "We've had an invite to introduce a band on stage in Bradford and hang with them after. Some guy called Reever or Reeves or something like that. I think he said the band's called Tin Men or Tin Pot Men? Have you ever heard of them?"

WITH DAVID BOWIE AND TIN MACHINE

THIS TIME OUT FRONT COVER HELPED LAUNCH THE CAREER OF THE BAILEY BROTHERS

Dez: "No kid, I have heard of Tin Machine, Bowie's band."

Mick: "That's it, Tin Machine, oh shit, he gave me a number to call and I'm saying yeah, ok yeah and never wrote it down, thought it was a windup."

Well after a few harsh words and a brotherly row, I hung up. An hour later Mick rings me.

Mick: "You are never gonna guess who's just called me? David Bowie, I knew it was him, no mistaking that voice. He said

"Mick its David, I know you think it's a wind up but we've been recording our album in Switzerland, every week we stop for an hour and watch your MTV show. We love it. My grandparents are from Doncaster and it's great to hear a Yorkshire accent on the TV. We are playing up north not far from you guys and we would love you to come and hang with us, introduce us on to the stage. It would be nice to meet you guys."

The rest as they say, is history. We met David who was so friendly; he introduced us to all the band and as promised we went on stage at the St Georges Hall. We had a good banter with the Bradford audience before introducing David Bowie and Tin Machine on stage. Bowie also invited us back to the hotel to hang after the show which was cool of him.

During Bowie's performance we were approached by ITV who had filmed us, they wanted us to come to the studio to be interviewed that week. They did a big feature on us including using live clips on stage to over a hundred thousand rock fans at the Monsters Of Rock festival. You expect to run into rock bands doing the circuit we were on but Bowie was a different league. It will go down as one of our career highlights for sure.

Ronnie James Dio:

'Richie Blackmore's Rainbow' (1975) and 'Rainbow Rising' (1976) - those two albums take us back to the mid-'70s when we first came across the amazing vocal and song writing prowess of Ronnie James Dio.

He had great stage presence and interaction with his audience. We always got on well with Ronnie; he did a great radio show trailer for the 'Bailey Brothers Rock Show' before we interviewed him. Can remember once in London, his wife and manager Wendy Dio inviting us to dine with them at a plush hotel, Savoy or something. Anyway, we were looking at the menu and it's like a week's wage for a bowl of soup to a northerner. A typical Michelin stared restaurant, Wendy could see us

With Ronnie James Dio

transfixed at the menu with sheer fright and politely said "Hey guys you're our guests, this is on us". We still ordered the cheapest thing on there because we don't take the piss. Well it came out like a work of art, the presentation was amazing, the problem was that the portions were like kids' size, three mouthfuls and it was gone. The bill for this small gathering was well over a thousand pounds - ouch!

Two hours later Mick and I were in the curry house because we were still hungry. Sat behind us was guitar legend Jeff Beck who gave us a friendly greeting. One thing about London you never know who you are gonna bump into!

EDDIE VAN HALEN:

After hearing the 1978 "Van Halen" release on Warner Brothers like many we were hooked. Eddie was one of the most influential guitarist since Hendrix. He inspired generations of guitar players, combined musicality with a stunningly effective range of techniques. A gifted song writer, he was also innovative in his engineering, always searching for the tone. His tapping technique became his trade mark and throughout the '80s you could hear his influence on album after album of wanna be guitar heroes. We will miss his smile, his amazing tone, his guitar playing, song writing, showmanship and his ability to raise the bar. A legend isn't a strong enough statement; he is beyond a title. Just gutted

RIP Eddie x

LAST WORD... WHAT GOES AROUND COMES AROUND...

Mick Bailey said: When Def Leppard come to town it's almost a given we are going to be there. I decided to call into Starbucks with my partner Mary-anne, the next minute I get a tap on the shoulder "Mick from the famous Bailey Brothers". It's only Phil Collen himself having a coffee before the gig tonight. He sat down with us and says to his friend "This is Mick from the Bailey Brothers. We go right back to the Girl days and the Retford Porterhouse" I was really surprised to see him in public so close to a live show but it shows how humble he is. It was also worth noting that he remembered us gigging together before we were called the Bailey Brothers. Girl were a cool band at that time fronted by Phil Lewis. Phil Collen invited us back stage after the show to hang and was genuinely pleased to meet up again.
After all the fame and fortune it's still only about the music and the people. Proud of Leppard still playing arenas - say no more.

A STAR IN THE MAKING -MICK'S SON MJ

Crossfire Eagles – one to watch say the Bailey Brothers.

It's pretty ironic that when the young band Crossfire Eagles featuring Tyler Savage - son of Def Leppard's Rick Savage - needed somewhere to play live it was Firepit Rocks on West Street that provided the venue (and chicken wings). Owned by Dez's son Rick, he has put the band on several times. When Tyler Savage saw pictures all over the venue of the Bailey Brothers and Def Leppard together, he took photos on his phone and sent it to his dad Rick Savage who was on tour with Leppard. Crossfire Eagles seemed to want to put on a good show for us and later said," We were a bit nervous knowing you guys were watching us"!

Crossfire Eagles with Mick, Dez and Rick Bailey

Rising stars of the tribute world - South Yorkshire's Billion Dollar Alice

The author

Sheffield-born Neil Anderson has written on music and entertainment for titles spanning the Independent to the Big Issue.

His original ***'Signing On For The Devil'*** became a best-seller and helped inspire his **www.dirtystopouts.com** operation that is an ever-evolving celebration of retro after dark entertainment.

Author Neil Anderson

Acknowledgements:

Rachael Hope and her 'I used to go to Rebels in Sheffield' Facebook Group that helped kick this whole project off, Sheffield Newspapers for use of their wonderful pics and articles, Sheffield City Council, Olga Marshall, The Bailey Brothers, Paul Unwin, Pete Gill, Andy Smith, Phil Staniland, Bitter Suite, Jane Salt, Graham Walker, Steve Baxendale, George Webster, Paul and Tracy Mirfin at The Casbah (formerly the Wapentake Bar), Mark 'DJ Mutley' Hobson (not forgetting his Kiss Katz Mobile Disco), Steve Stevlor, Nigel Lockwood, Caroline Gowing, Eugene at Big Cheese/Vive Le Rock Magazine, Robbie Bifield, Chris Twiby, Janet Barker, Joe Elliott, Rick Savage, John Alflat, David Dunn, DJ Lez Wright, DJ Ken Hall, Steve 'DJ Rude Dog' Rodgers, Gerry Laffy, Phil Staniland, Graham Wild, Steve Wilcock, Ben Duke, Janet Barker, Libby Dry, Dom Bescoby, Lee Ford, Emma Bradbury, Spirit of the Wapentake, Sue Whitehead, Pete Willis, Graham Oliver, Steve Dawson, Andy Barker, Chris Calow, Glenn Marples, Marie Jenkinson, Bob Maltby, Mark Latham, Mark Burton, Iain and Mandi Barker, Dave Palfreyman, Buffy, Sally McLaugh- lan, Glenn Milligan, Mandy Jeffcock, Sue and Richard Gregory, Gary Holmes, Andy Barrott, Simon Hinkler, David Muscroft (www.davidmuscroft.com), Reprobate., Shirley Freeman, Mark Lindley, Sue Quinn, Helen Clark, Bill Stephenson, Paula Burgin, Pete Wood and John Stabler.

Are you ready to rock....
Again?
ROCK THE FUCKIN'
CASBAH
SHEFFIELD
REBELS
ROXY
ROCK NIGHT!
WAPENTAKE
SHEFFIELD
REBELS
SHEFFIELD
Available from www.dirtystopouts.com